LOST AND FOUND

L·O·S·T

AND

FOUND

...

JIM LEHRER

G. P. PUTNAM'S SONS

New York

G. P. Putnam's Sons
Publishers Since 1838
200 Madison Avenue
New York, NY 10016

Library of Congress Cataloging-in-Publication Data

Lehrer, James.
Lost and found / Jim Lehrer.
p.   cm.
I. Title.
ISBN 0-399-13601-0
PS3562.E4419L67   1991   90-46015 CIP
813' .54—dc20

Printed in the United States of America
1   2   3   4   5   6   7   8   9   10

This book is printed on acid-free paper.

Always, for Kate

. . .

1
. . .
RUNAWAY
LUTHER

LUTHER WALLACE, the speaker of our Oklahoma House of Representatives, said good-bye to his wife, Annabel, at their house in the Nichols Hills section of Oklahoma City at 7:25 A.M. He drove off as always in his yellow Pontiac Firebird, but he never arrived at his office in the state capitol twenty-one blocks away.

His secretary and legislative assistants did not begin to concern themselves until after ten o'clock. He had told them he would be late because of a breakfast meeting he had with me and some others about the Turnpike Mess. Several legislators were locked tight in battle with the governor over who should have a new turnpike running to their hometowns. Mess was what the Oklahoma City and Tulsa newspapers called it, and they were dead right. The last things Oklahoma needed right then were more turnpikes to anywhere.

Luther's staff got restless after they called my office and found out that I had not had breakfast and that the turn-pike meeting was tomorrow, not today. Annabel did not concern herself until after lunch, when somebody from his office finally called to ask if she knew where Luther was.

C. Harry Hayes and the agents of the Oklahoma Bureau of Investigation were not notified until almost two-thirty in the afternoon. C. told me, the lieutenant governor. I informed the governor, who joked about the Republicans dancing in the streets of Tulsa by nightfall. Luther, the governor and I were all Democrats, like Jimmy Carter, who was then president of the United States.

The decision was made to keep it a secret from the press and everybody else in Oklahoma until either he showed up or more was known.

Everyone expected him to turn up any minute.

He did not.

So at four o'clock C. had OBI agents quietly check all hospitals and jails in the area. No Luther. All parking lots at or near airports, bus stations and train stations were scanned for his yellow Pontiac Firebird. Nothing. C. ordered a retracing of what should have been Luther's route from his house to the capitol. Luther was usually noticed, because he was a big shot and because he was in a yellow car that came by at about the same time every morning. A Mexican-American kid at an Exxon station on North-west 63rd Street remembered seeing him. So did an older guy who ran a car wash on 63rd closer to Nichols Hills.

But that was it. Nobody after the turn onto Lincoln Boulevard had seen that yellow car. So C. figured that instead of turning right as usual at Lincoln and going south the last forty or so blocks to the capitol, Luther kept going another two miles to the freeway, Interstate 35, which also ran north and south.

The question was, Did he turn right and head to downtown Oklahoma City and/or points south, or did he swing left toward Guthrie and/or points north?

And most important, why? Was somebody in the car with him with a gun to his head? Was it possible that the speaker of the Oklahoma House of Representatives had been kidnapped? Or worse?

Or less.

·   ·   ·

C. asked me to go with him to see Annabel. He had already talked to her on the phone, but he had not put any tough questions or propositions to her. Now he had to and he did not want to do it by himself. Just smile when I frown, he said. Be soft when I'm rough, he said.

Yes, sir, I said.

C. Harry Hayes was my friend. He and I had been through several adventures together, some official, some unofficial. We were drawn together by several things, but mostly we just liked each other's company. Every male needs at least one male to tell the truth to, and we were each other's. If you've got a brother or a father or an uncle or somebody at the plant or office or in the neighborhood, that's fine. Neither C. nor I had any of those. We also had being deformed in common. He had only one ear, having lost his right one in a shooting-range accident when he was a rookie cop in Durant. I had only one eye, having lost my left one when a can was kicked up in my face while I was watching a kick-the-can game years ago growing up in Kansas.

"I get the impression she's not the brightest person in the world," C. said of Annabel Wallace as we turned off 63rd into Nichols Hills. "Pretty is about all there is, right?"

"Right," I said almost automatically, without thinking. "I guess. Right."

"Well, she's no Jackie, that's for sure."

That was for sure. Jackie was my wife. The founder and chairman of JackieMarts Inc., the nation's first and largest chain of drive-thru grocery stores. She was smart, opinionated, articulate and very much her own person separate from the wife of the lieutenant governor—the Second Lady of Oklahoma.

C. asked me exactly what I knew about Annabel Wallace. I told him she was the kind of politician's wife that always made me very sad. She and Luther had grown up oil-rich together in Newtonville, gone to high school together and then off to OU and then to the altar after he'd returned from a famous law school in Massachusetts. She'd stepped aside for him and law school, for him and his political career, for him and everything. I had not been around her that much, but I could not remember ever having a conversation with her about anything that mattered. Anything other than the day's high or overnight low temperature, where our children were in school and how they were doing, and family vacation plans.

"Is she a crier?" C. asked.

"I cannot imagine her crying," I said. "It's not allowed, except at funerals, where it's required."

She met us at the door in a light purple silk dress and black patent high heels, as if she were going to a ladies' luncheon instead of a talk about her missing husband. She was still a gorgeous woman despite her age. Which was probably the same as Luther's, which I knew was some-where in the late forties. She had been a tall thin blonde, but now she was a tall thin dyed-white blonde. Not a thing was out of place on her head or her face. Jackie would have said she was too fixed, but I figured Annabel would not have even known what being too fixed was.

The house was a sandy brick mansion that resembled one of those main lodges at a lake resort. It went off in various levels and layers in all directions with wall-to-wall white and beige shag carpeting and furniture that mostly was white trimmed in gold. She took us into a room that had a white grand piano, hundreds of photo-graphs in silver frames, bookshelves that went all of the way to the ceiling, and small bronze sculptures of cowboys riding horses like the ones at the National Cowboy Hall of Fame there in Oklahoma City.

She and C. sat down side by side on a long red-flowered couch. I sat right across a mammoth glass coffee table from them in a matching overstuffed chair.

We declined Annabel's offer of a refreshment or snack.

"First, let me report, Mrs. Wallace, that we have not turned up any information about the Speaker's where-abouts," C. said, softly, politely. "Because of the need for discretion we have, of course, not yet vigorously pursued the matter."

Annabel said nothing. Her face was stuck in a half-smile. Like it would always be stuck in a half-smile.

"I assume you have heard nothing as well?" C. continued.

"That's correct," she said.

"Have you come up with any ideas or thoughts about what might have happened?" he said, ever so gently. "Anything at all, no matter how . . ."

"Nothing. I have no idea where he is or what has happened to him."

"Would you mind if I asked you a series of questions? Some of them may seem a bit harsh, but it would be most helpful in planning our approach to pursuing the matter."

Just the smile, an affirmative nod and the word "Certainly."

"Was the Speaker in any difficulty of any kind? Personal, professional—any kind at all?"

"Not that I know of."

"No financial problems?"

"None."

"Was he on the outs with anybody? Anybody who might have said something of a threatening nature?"

"As Mack knows, politicians are always on the outs with people. The other night Luther told me somebody was probably going to kill him over this turnpike mess if he didn't kill them first. But that's the nature of the business, right, Mack?" she laughed.

"Right, Annabel," I said.

"Did he seem worried or concerned about anything but maybe without having told you what it was about?"

"No."

"No family crises?"

"None now. None, really, ever."

"You have how many children?"

"Four. All are grown and happy and no problem to their parents. I've called them to see if they might have heard anything from him. They hadn't. I hope I didn't get them all upset. They'll all be here as soon as they can. Unless he . . . well, unless he is found. Luther has been a great father to them. . . ."

"As you have been a great mother," I said.

"Thank you, Mack. I have tried. That's all any of us can do."

C. let a couple of beats of silence sink in before he said: "Now, a difficult question. But I feel I must ask it. Please understand that I am asking only because it might be helpful in leading us to clear up this situation."

The half-smile remained. She knew what was coming. So did I.

"Did your husband have a female interest outside the marriage?" C. said, his voice so quiet I could barely hear him from across the glass table.

"Certainly not," she said. "We love each other very

much. Luther is a faithful husband. I know he is. I just know it."

"Yes, ma'am. Please understand why I had to ask. . . ."

"I understand." It was clear she did not understand. Never in a thousand years would it have occurred to her that one day a pair of deformed men would be sitting in her lovely living room in Nichols Hills asking her about whether her husband, the speaker of the Oklahoma House, was playing around.

"Did the two of you quarrel recently?"

"No."

"Did he indicate in any way any unhappiness?"

There was a slight glance away from C. Half a beat. "No. Luther was one of the happiest persons I have ever known. Wouldn't you say so, too, Mack?"

"Good point, Annabel," I said. "I would agree."

C. pressed on: "Did he say anything, no matter how indirectly, about leaving?"

"Not a word."

"Would you mind if we checked your bank account to see if there have been any recent withdrawals?"

There was that glance away again. But the smile remained. "Certainly not. We have accounts at the First National and at Oklahoma Bank and Trust."

"Thank you," C. said. "Do you know if any unknown or unusual people contacted him lately?"

"No. Just the usual assortment from the legislature and people around the state who wanted Luther to do something for them." She laughed. So did C. and I.

"Has he been on any unusual trips lately?"

"Just to a reunion with some old Marine friends," she said. And laughed again. "I didn't go and he didn't say much about it. It was in Kansas City, so that would make it unusual, I guess. He went with a businessman named Bob Thornton from down in Pawnee City. They were in together."

I knew all about Luther's being a Marine. Everybody who talked to him for more than fifteen minutes or so did. He'd been an infantry officer, a lieutenant, in the late fifties, and he loved to talk about it.

C., who had been holding a small red spiral notebook, closed it and stood up. "Well, thank you so much, Mrs. Wallace. I am sorry I had to barge in like this. But I felt it was important to get as early a start as possible."

She led us back to the front door.

"The difficulty from now on," C. said, "is keeping this under wraps. Several people now know of it. I must notify the FBI, the highway patrol and all the local police departments. It won't be long before it gets out to the press. It will be a very big story, as I am sure you know. I will have a plainclothes officer outside your house here twenty-four hours a day. Please feel free to call upon him to keep anybody away you want kept away. I would also like your permission to begin telephone surveillance."

She didn't know what he meant. "To have all calls here automatically monitored at our office," he said. "In case someone tries to contact you about the Speaker."

"Whatever you feel you must do," she said. "But I'm sure . . . well, whatever you feel you must do."

Annabel shook C.'s hand and thanked him. Then she

turned to me and grabbed my right hand with both of hers. "This must be tough on you, too, Mack," she said. "Luther considers you one of his best friends."

We were barely at the car before C. said: "I didn't know you and Luther were *that* close."

"I like him, you know that," I replied. "He's fun and smart."

In the middle of the next block, I asked C. for his best guesses.

"He was on the take from some road contractor or some such. It was about to come out, so he ran away, probably to put a shotgun in his mouth.

"He was getting it off with some young Oklahoma maiden, and she got pregnant and blackmailed him into running off with her to Mexico or some such exotic place.

"He was kidnapped by somebody wanting some of his family's money, or something from the State of Oklahoma, as ransom.

"He had a nervous breakdown as a result of his mentally taxing work as the leader of the Oklahoma House of Representatives and strayed over the border into Arkansas, where he was mugged by a hillbilly.

"Whatever, we'll know soon."

I asked: "Why soon? How soon?"

"We always know within a few hours. Nobody just disappears without a trace. Particularly a nobody like the speaker of our House."

It was more than just a play with words. C. had never been as fond of Luther as I was. He said he was too smart

by half to be running the Oklahoma House of Representatives, for one thing. And Luther knew it, for another.
The best thing about him, C. always said, was that he
was the only one in Oklahoma who could scare sanity
into our governor, Joe Hayman. Sometimes.

· · ·

The turnpike meeting the next morning was in the
Sparrow Room, a private dining room at the Park Plaza
Hotel downtown. All of the meeting rooms there were
named for birds. The man who called the meeting, Ron
Worthen, had picked the place and the participants.
He was a retired orthopedic surgeon from Muskogee who
was chairman of the Oklahoma Turnpike Authority. I
was there representing Governor Joe Hayman. There
were three others: the Senate majority leader, the chairman of the state highway and roads commission, and the
executive director of the Turnpike Authority.

We sat at a round table. There was one empty chair—
Luther's place. We ate our breakfast of green melon,
scrambled eggs, sausage patties, biscuits and coffee without
him. There were some comments about his being late, but
nobody much minded until it was time to get down to
business. It took some doing, but I finally got Worthen
to proceed without Luther, on the grounds that we were
all busy people with other appointments on our schedules
for the day and that I would make it my responsibility
to make sure Luther was fully briefed.

Worthen said it was so unlike the Speaker to forget or
otherwise miss a meeting. I agreed but said there was

always the first time for everything. Or something brilliant like that.

Worthen asked the Turnpike Authority director to review the situation. His name was Travis Ritter. He was a tall loose man in his late thirties who had played second-string forward on the OSU team that had won conference a few years back.

"We have just completed a traffic count," he said, getting right down to business. "Neither one of these proposed routes needs a turnpike. They barely need the two-lane highways they have now, to be perfectly frank. Look at these figures."

He held up a yard-square piece of white poster board with numbers on it in red crayon. Red and white, OU colors.

"On the Adabel–Sturant proposal. Twenty-three miles. The existing route, State Highway Ninety-seven. Weekdays, on average, a hundred two car trips westbound, a hundred five eastbound . . ."

"Why more one way than the other?" I asked, making mischief.

"Some people go east and never return," said Bill Haden of Sallisaw, the Senate majority leader. "Maybe you could get the governor to appoint a commission to find out where those people are going—and why? Maybe they're dropping off the edge of Oklahoma into a black hole of Arkansas or something."

It gave us all a laugh. Ritter continued with his chart and his words and numbers.

"We estimate that it would cost ten million dollars to build a regular four-lane road over those twenty-three miles. At the CTR—car-trip rate—I just outlined, at fifty cents a car it would take over a hundred years to retire the debt. No bond house would ever issue revenue bonds on that kind of projection."

"So you are telling us what we already know," said Haden of Sallisaw, no friend of Joe Hayman, whom he had opposed once for the Democratic nomination for governor. "It's an insane idea. We already knew that. I assume the other one is the same?"

"Yes, sir," said Ritter, pulling out another poster-board chart headed NOWATA–VINITA. "It's the same, only worse. It would take a hundred twenty-five years to retire the bonds for that twenty-eight-mile masterpiece. Its car-trip count is down in the eighties both ways."

"Call Joe off of it, Mack," Haden said to me. "It's ridiculous. I know Luther feels the same way, because he's already told me and everyone else who'll listen. Tell Joe Luther's ready to fight him to the end on it, too."

"Luther's told me and Joe that, too," I said. "But so far Joe's set in concrete on this. He will be hard to move...."

"He's set in something smellier than concrete," Haden said, standing up. "I know the pressures on him, but when he gets back from Buffalo tell him again it's a loser. It takes both the House and the Senate to approve new turnpikes, and I can tell you it ain't going to happen no matter what Joe and his friends Hank and Jerry J. want. The people are already laughing their asses off about it and I have no intention of their laughing mine off with them. If Luther was here he'd say the same thing. Only louder and better."

Hank was Hank Lawter, the state senator from Sturant who was owed a huge political debt by Joe and who was pushing one of the turnpikes. Jerry J. was Jerry J. Chandler of Nowata, one of Joe's major campaign contributors, who was pushing the other one.

We did not linger over coffee. I went on to my office at the capitol.

Joe had gone to Buffalo, his hometown in the Panhandle, the night before to attend the funeral of an uncle. I had a couple of days at least to deal with it—him.

• • •

I had been at the office less than an hour when the note arrived. Janice Alice Montgomery, my lovely old lady secretary, marched into my office with it in one hand and a Mexican-American kid by the collar in the other. He was about eighteen. He had delivered it and left, but when Janice Alice had seen what it was she had sent one of the capitol policemen running after him.

The boy was dressed in a blue Exxon service station uniform. The note was from Luther. It was handwritten in black ballpoint pen on his personal stationery, on which was printed in heavy blue ink at the top: THE SPEAKER.

The note said:

Mack—

I have gone away and I did it completely on my own accord. I have not been kidnapped or anything like that. I am not in danger and I am not crazy. Please tell Hayes and the police not to look for me, because they'd never find me. But even if they did I will not return until I am good and ready and that might be never. I have committed no crime so there is no way to make me come back. I am sorry it had to be this way. My family will be fine without me. So will the House and the people of Oklahoma.

My best always,
Luther

The kid's name was Daniel Gomez. He said Luther, whom he knew because he bought gas at the Exxon station and waved every morning on the way to the capitol, had wheeled in there the morning before and paid him $200 to hide the yellow car in a garage behind the station and deliver the note this morning at nine. Gomez said Luther told him he was playing a practical joke on me. That was the reason Gomez had not told the OBI agent about it the afternoon before. He said Luther had left the station a few minutes later in a taxi. He said he had no idea where Luther was going.

• • •

OBI agents found Luther's car right where Gomez had said it was. After some skepticism, C. and I ended up believing his story. C. even let Gomez keep the $200, particularly after the taxi driver who had driven Luther away from the Exxon was located.

The driver said he had taken Luther downtown to the Sheraton Park Hotel. But there the trail ended. Nobody remembered checking Luther in, waiting on him or seeing him. C.'s theory was that Luther had walked in the front door and probably right out the back, and gotten into another car.

And gone far, far away.

Wherever, he'd gone, he'd gone with money. It turned out Luther had withdrawn $50,000 in cash from the Oklahoma Bank and Trust the afternoon before. Most of it was in $500 and $100 bills. He'd told the bank president, a friend, he was going to give it to Annabel as a birthday present, with a note for her to buy a new red convertible of her choice. He told the banker Annabel had always wanted a red convertible and now she was going to have one. The banker, an uptight, slick-haired Republican named Randall, told C. he had no reason to doubt or question, because Luther had more than $300,000 in various accounts at the bank.

Luther had made no withdrawals from any of his accounts in any other banks. So, wherever he'd gone, he'd gone with $50,000 in cash.

C. asked me to go with him to tell Annabel about the money and show her the note. She had the same smile and took us to the same room, where we sat in the same places.

The smile broke for an instant when she read his note. But just for an instant. "I wish he had said something to me as well," she said. And that was all she said.

Her reaction to the $50,000 withdrawal was similar. "That won't last him very long."

It was clear that only one emotion was driving her now: anger. She was mad at Luther. He had run out on her without a word. He had embarrassed her before these two deformed men and would soon embarrass her before the world of her friends and all of Oklahoma. He had run away.

C. asked her if she had, by chance, checked Luther's belongings? Was anything missing? Like a suitcase, some clothes? His razor? Toothbrush?

"Nothing except his passport," she said.

Oh my, I thought.

"Oh my," C. said. "Had he any favorite places to go overseas?"

"No. We never went on vacation overseas. Luther thought it would look bad to the people of Oklahoma for their speaker to vacation in London or Paris or wherever. So we went to New Orleans, around Corpus Christi down on the Texas coast, and places around here like Lake Murray and a lodge over in the Kiamichi Mountains."

"Why did he have a passport, then?"

"He said he needed one to go to an international meeting of state legislative leaders in Mexico next month."

That rang a bell with me. I said: "It's across the border in Nuevo Laredo. Luther told me it was the first time he had ever been anywhere foreign since the Marine Corps."

"Where was he in the Marines?" C. asked Annabel.

"Mostly in the Far East," she said. "Okinawa, the Philippines, Japan."

C. gave her three or four more opportunities to volunteer information. He even asked her point blank for her best guess as to where Luther had gone and why.

Each time she just shook her head and said something like, "I have no idea."

I had the feeling she was telling the truth.

Back at the car, C. said what I already knew: "You don't need a passport to go to Nuevo Laredo."

· · ·

Auditors went over a few books in the Speaker's office to see whether any petty-cash money was missing. None was. Some discreet checks were made around the capitol to see if any women employees had also suddenly dropped out of sight. None had. C. had some of his agents check "sources" in Oklahoma City's very small homosexual community. Nothing. Luther was not one of them. No airline passenger list on any flight out of Oklahoma City that missing morning or since had Luther's name on it. No airline employee remembered seeing him. Similar checks at the Amtrak station, the bus depot and all of the car rental places in town turned up the same result.

As each day went by, we all wondered if this would be the day a reporter for *The Daily Oklahoman* or some

Channel XYZ or another stumbled across the fact that Luther had run away from home.

On Day Four, C. and I discussed the advisability of advising Annabel or somebody simply to announce it.

"How about this for the announcement," I said in my best lieutenant-governor deep voice. " 'Ladies and gentlemen of the Oklahoma press. We have summoned you here today to announce the disappearance of Luther Wallace, our beloved speaker of the House. He dropped out of sight like a rock in a puddle a few days ago. He told nobody where he was going and we have no idea where he went. All we know is that he took fifty thousand dollars in cash with him. There is no evidence of foul play, no evidence of any crime having been committed by him or anyone else. He just went away. Are there any questions?' "

"One of us could leak it, you know," C. said. "Call Smitty at the *Oklahoman*. We'd own him for life."

"That is a disgusting idea," I said.

C. and I were having lunch, C. style, in the backseat of his black Lincoln OBI command car. For a long time C., who wore nothing but gray suits, ate nothing for lunch except hamburgers from McDonald's and Burger King. But then he discovered pizza. Pizza is an Italian pie kind of thing with cheese, tomato sauce and various toppings all baked together on a thin piece of round dough. It apparently was known and popular for years in the North and East, but it had come only in the last few years to Oklahoma. Today we had gone through the drive-thru at a Pizza Throne just up Lincoln Boulevard from the capitol. C. had his usual, a small with green peppers and sausage, and a carton of milk. I got a Dr Pepper to drink with my small pizza with pepperoni. Pepperoni is like midget bologna. It's about the size of a quarter and it's hotter. They cut it paper-thin.

"Annabel Wallace has hired Jack Cartwright to sort all of it out," C. said. Cartwright was a leading Oklahoma City lawyer who charged an arm and a leg just to say hello on the phone. His main business was suing the government on behalf of oil companies. "I told him everything I know. Which is that thus far it looks like Luther was just as straight and square and decent as he appeared to be."

"You're not doing anything more to look for him, are you?" I asked.

"Not officially."

"What does that mean?"

We were both talking with our mouths full of pizza, with red tomato sauce dripping down on us and our napkins. I longed for the good old days of Big Macs and Whoppers.

"It means I want to know what happened. The stories about this are going to be wild with speculation and lies."

"It can't last too long, because there is nothing to report," I said. "He just ran away."

"Grown men who are successful politicians do not just run away, Mack. Grown men who are successful anythings do not just run away."

"Right," I said.

Right.

C. asked me about the turnpikes. Was Buffalo Joe, or The Chip as C. called him, going to back down? Had he come to his senses? Please, please, Mr. Lieutenant Governor, tell me all.

I told C. all I knew. Which was that I had reported to the governor fully about my breakfast meeting with Bill Haden and the others. I had told him about the CTRs and the bonds and what Haden had said about what his feet were really set in.

"There are two ways to fight," Joe had responded. "Scared and smart, and scared and stupid. I don't believe I have to tell you how we will fight, do I, Mack? Do I?"

"No, Joe."

"Remember that, Mack. We did not get to be the First and Second Men of Oklahoma by being scared and stupid."

"Joe, I owe you my best judgment, and I am sorry to say that I think the other side is right this time. Neither one of those turnpikes makes one ounce of sense at all."

Joe was a big man who wore mostly dark brown suits, white shirts and black ties. His hair was wavy dark brown. In other words, he looked like a buffalo as well as being from Buffalo. Which made the nickname "Buffalo Joe" stick like true glue. C.'s nickname for him came from "buffalo chip," as in buffalo dung.

"That, of course, is not the issue, is it?" Joe had said without blinking, as if I had just passed on to him a recipe for chili dogs or something.

"Remind me again what the issue is, Joe," I had said.

We were standing in the small anteroom outside his office and he was making it increasingly clear with his famous good-bye smile that this meeting was over.

"Friendship, Mack. I promised my friends they could have turnpikes, and I deliver on my promises to my friends. Show me somebody who doesn't and I'll show you a somebody who is soon to be a nobody."

C. loved Joe stories. He was so enthralled with this one that he forgot to wipe his mouth regularly. It and his chin were covered with tomato sauce when I finished. It made me gag.

And it made me so wish and pray again for the speedy return of hamburgers and fries to my life with C. in the fast-food lane.

. . .

The story got out while we were eating our pizza. C. let me out of his car in the parking lot on the west side of the capitol building. I was only four or five steps in the door and down the hallway toward the elevator when a young woman radio reporter from Tulsa screeched up to me with both her tape recorder and her mouth wide open. "The Speaker's disappeared! The Speaker's disappeared! What's your comment?"

I told her I had no comment and suggested she contact Jack Cartwright's office.

It kicked up quite a storm. Understandably. The Mysterious Disappearance of Speaker Wallace was all over the television news programs that evening and it was banner news on the front pages of every daily newspaper in Oklahoma the next morning. Annabel Wallace was unavailable for any comment. Cartwright did all of the talking. He said the family did not know of Luther Wallace's whereabouts and they were worried about his safety. He said Luther had never disappeared before and there was no history of mental illness in Luther or his family. C. was quoted saying thus far there was no evidence of kidnapping, murder or any other kind of foul play and there was no evidence the Speaker was fleeing the probability of any arrest or revelation concerning his own conduct—personal, political or professional. C. also released the contents of Luther's note to me.

The house majority leader was the second in command of the House. He was a regional butane gas dealer from Mangum who said he would assume—with a saddened but hopeful heart—the duties of speaker until Luther reappeared or until the House convened in January to elect a new one. Whichever came first. Meanwhile, he remained in Mangum.

The story stayed alive and dominant everywhere for the next several days, until the press tired of reporting the simple and inescapable fact that there was nothing more to report.

Luther Wallace had run away from home. From Oklahoma. He was lost. What else was there to say? Or to do about it?

2

. . .

MUD PIES

AFTER about five weeks it was almost like Luther Wallace had never existed. There was nothing to report, so there were no stories about him anymore. The major drama of Oklahoma moved on to the coming of the Great Turnpike Shootout between the governor and the legislature. I began to go whole days without hearing anybody mention Luther or wonder out loud whatever in the world he had done with himself. Because he was assumed still to be alive, there wasn't even a funeral or a memorial service to plan, attend or critique. The House majority leader came to Oklahoma City twice and walked into Luther's office and asked if there was anything to do. No, replied Luther's secretary and assistants, and the House majority leader issued a statement against the turnpikes and returned to Mangum.

C. said he was still nosing around, but not only had he not turned up any facts or leads, he was also fresh out of theories. None on that original guess list of his had panned out. Yet.

Then I traveled to Pawnee City down in the southern part of the state.

I went to dedicate a new Sears mall. It wasn't till I got there and found that I had some time to kill before heading back to Oklahoma City that I remembered Luther's friend Bob Thornton. He lived in Pawnee City. He and Luther had served in the Marines together. Didn't Annabel say he was a businessman of some kind?

It took one stop at the chamber of commerce to find that Bob Thornton was manager of the downtown SSO store. "SSO" stood for "Sooner State Optical." There were hundreds of SSOs all over the state. A man named Fats Ragsdale had started them several years before to bring affordable eyeglasses to the people of Oklahoma. I had represented the governor and the state government at Fats's funeral in Oklahoma City a few years before. They called him Fats because he weighed 350 pounds and was a gambler.

The SSO was on the courthouse square. It was a thin slice out of a storefront that had once been a big department store or a Woolworth's and was now three stores. The other two were vacant. Probably because of the mall I had just blessed in the name of the State of Oklahoma. I hated what those ugly things were doing to our downtowns and courthouse squares. It wasn't just Pawnee City. It was everywhere. It used to be that there was never anybody downtown after dark. Now there wasn't anybody there in the daytime, either. I hated it, and yet there I'd been, cutting another red-and-white ribbon for another Killer Mall.

There were two people in the SSO. A woman behind the small glass counter of glasses frames and cases, and a woman customer. Both were in their late forties or so and comfortable with one another. They knew each other. Friends, maybe. The customer was trying on sunglasses.

A bell tinkled when I opened the door. The place was narrow and full of mirrors and colored photographs and drawings of beautiful tanned women and handsome tanned men wearing glasses. The woman behind the counter smiled and came right to me. "Well, hello, may I help you?" she said. She was wearing glasses herself. Good red plastic frames around pudgy oval lenses. Her face was also pudgy, and it was also open and friendly.

"Is Bob Thornton here?" I asked.

I heard the sound of a pair of sunglasses hitting the glass counter. The customer had dropped them. The clerk glanced over at the other woman. So did I.

"No," said the clerk. "No, he isn't." Her voice wavered. Just a bit. Like talking through water. Her eyes contracted. Her face was closing in.

I made my voice as friendly as I could. And kept going. "Will he be back today?"

"No . . . well, probably not. No."

"Then I will call in the morning. He will certainly be here by then, right?"

"Yes, sir. Probably. Yes, sir. Who shall I say was calling?

35

You're not from SSO in Oklahoma City, are you?" Her eyes cut over toward the customer. She just couldn't help it.

"No."

She did not know I was lieutenant governor of Oklahoma, obviously. Nobody ever recognized me as lieutenant governor of Oklahoma. And right then something made me decide not to tell her.

"Tell him one of his old Marine buddies came by."

It was as if she were a bicycle tube and I had let her air out. Whoosh.

"Were you at the Kansas City reunion?" she asked. She was anxious. She wanted me to have been there.

"I wasn't able to make it."

"Is the Marines where you lost your eye?" It was a nervous-reaction question. Something to keep the conversation going.

"No, ma'am."

"Have you thought about a glass eye? Mr. Thornton knows how to order them. Some place in Ohio makes some really attractive ones. I swear you can hardly tell the difference between them and the real. They put a little wire somewhere up there, too, so it moves like a real one when the other one moves."

I excused myself and headed toward the door.

"What did you say your name was?" she said. "I'll tell Mr. Thornton you were here. . . ."

"Tom Bell Pepper Bowen," I replied, closing the door behind me.

Tom Bell Pepper Bowen had been a U.S. Marine and

my best friend. He'd died a hero in the Korean War. His widow, Jackie, was now married to me.

· · ·

The phone book gave me the address. A young man with a map at a Texaco station told me how to find it. It was a one-story brick house with an attached garage. In an Oklahoma City newspaper real estate ad it would have been listed as a three-bedroom rambler. I pulled up into the driveway. There was no sign of life. There was no answer at the front door. I peeked in a window at what was obviously the living room. It looked like it had been a while since anybody had been inside. Everything about the place, including the yard and the smell, made it look like it had been a while since anybody had been inside.

I walked next door to a house almost exactly like the Thorntons'. The woman there told me that the Thorntons were both gone and that she was taking care of the mail and newspapers. She said Bob Thornton had left first, rather suddenly, and his wife had left two and a half to three weeks later. She said Mrs. Thornton, whose name was Sarah, had seemed very upset after her husband left, and was in tears and, shaking, had finally left herself. She had not said where she was going.

"I thought I saw just now that their SSO on the square is still open for business," I said.

"Sarah's sister is running it. I've been in there asking about Bob and Sarah. That sister just says they went away for a while on vacation. I don't believe it, but then what business is it of mine? Who did you say you were?"

"Tom Bowen," I replied. "I'm in insurance."

"Well, then get away from me. I have too much of that already."

"One last question," I said. "Do you happen to remember the exact day Mr. Thornton left?"

She looked at me and my one eye for a couple of beats. Should I or shouldn't I? Finally she said, "Hold on." She disappeared for a few minutes and then returned with a diary-type book. She leafed through it.

"It was the day before I had to go over to Pauls Valley to the chiropractor. That was on October sixth, so that means he must have left on October fifth. Now that's it. Scat, Mr. Insurance Man."

"Yes, ma'am."

October 5 was the day Luther Wallace had disappeared.

. . .

Well, well, I thought, as I headed for U.S. 70 and Oklahoma City. Two men attend a Marine reunion in Kansas City and a few weeks later both disappear. Well, well.

There was a Kerr-McGee station right ahead, so I decided to call C. immediately and tell him what I had found. And what I had figured out. It could wait until I got back, but why wait? I was a little bit like the boy with a report card full of A's wanting to show off to Daddy.

C.'s secretary came on the phone in a rush. "Oh, Mr. Lieutenant Governor, where are you? The director was looking everywhere for you," she said. "But he took off in the Cessna without you almost twenty minutes ago."

"Took off for where? What happened?"

"Oh, sir, there's been a terrible tragedy. A Continental Trailways bus went off the Red River Bridge south of Sturant. It was full of people. An awful thing."

"Who was the driver?"

"Who was the driver? My goodness, I don't know. It may be here in some notes. Yes, sir. Vermillion—T. Vermillion."

"Don't know him. I'm only forty or so minutes away from the bridge. I'll go right there."

"I'm sure the director would be so grateful to see you."

.   .   .

It was an anxious forty-minute drive. My mind traveled as fast as my three-year-old dark blue Buick Skylark.

I thought about that Red River Bridge that separated Texas from Oklahoma. I had been over it many times and I often wondered what it would be like to crash off of it into the river fifty feet below. As a matter of fact, I had never been able to drive over any bridge over any water without thinking morbid things like that. If nothing else, I always remembered the stories about people leaping off the Golden Gate Bridge in California and the Brooklyn Bridge in New York. Long, high bridges were spooky places to me.

I thought about it being a Continental Trailways bus. Buses were special. It had started back in Kansas when I was a kid, when I'd decided to become a ticket agent for Thunderbird Motor Coaches after I lost my left eye. It hadn't worked out then, but later in Oklahoma it did. I'd worked for a while in the Adabel bus depot before I went into politics and Thunderbird sold out to Continental. My bus interest had continued ever since, and I made a point of stopping by the Union Bus Station in Oklahoma City every so often just to see what was up and going on. I didn't know a T. Vermillion, because he was probably in the Sturant division, but I was on a first-name basis with several other drivers and ticket agents who worked in and out of Oklahoma City. My son had even worked in the Oklahoma City depot briefly as a baggage agent when he'd played semipro baseball for the Oklahoma Blue Arrow Motorcoaches team, the Buses. I'd been pushing him toward a career in buses, in fact, but it hadn't worked out. He'd gone into business for himself.

I had also encouraged Fred Rayburn, a driver with Oklahoma Blue Arrow Motorcoaches, to start his National Motor Coach Museum in Oklahoma City. It had not been terribly successful, but it was one of my favorite places to go. It was a great place to be alone: there was never anybody else there, because it was seldom open. But Fred had given me a key to go anytime I wished.

The highway patrol had closed the two southbound lanes of U.S. 69-75 a good two miles north of the bridge. There were two black-and-white trooper cars and three troopers in their two-tone brown uniforms at the roadblock. As I drove up to it, one of them motioned to me to turn left over the median stripe and go back the way I came. But I kept going, right up to him. His young face screwed up for confrontation.

"Didn't you see the signals? The road is closed," said

Trooper Kid in a voice of proud authority. He was only twenty-five or twenty-six. His dark brown straw campaign hat came down hard over his eyes, like he was practicing to be one of those Marine Corps drill instructors in the movies when he grew up. I wanted to tell him that my father was a lieutenant in the Kansas State Highway Patrol and I would probably have been a Kansas trooper myself if I hadn't become one-eyed. So why didn't he just relax and back off, please.

"I am the lieutenant governor of this state," I said. "I am to meet Director Hayes of the OBI at the scene of the accident."

His Mr. Tough expression did not change. "Do you have ID?"

"You mean a driver's license?" I was losing some patience now.

"ID that proves you are the lieutenant governor."

"They don't issue ID cards in this state for lieutenant governors, young man."

I gave him my driver's license and he went over to the two other troopers. I couldn't hear what they said, but each in turn shook his head. Obviously, neither knew the name or the face of the lieutenant governor of Oklahoma, either. So Trooper Kid slid into the front seat of one of the cars and talked into a two-way radio microphone.

After a while he returned to my car. He said, "Confirmed. You are the lieutenant governor of Oklahoma." Hallelujah! "Sorry for the inconvenience." He handed back my driver's license.

"You can't be too careful, can you, Trooper?" I said in a most sarcastic tone. "This road must be crawling with people posing as lieutenant governors of Oklahoma."

Trooper Kid did not change his expression or respond. "Just doing the job I swore on the Holy Bible to do, sir," he said. And he walked over and moved the wooden road barrier. I gunned my car on down the highway toward the Red River Bridge.

It was one of those times when I would not have minded if the lieutenant governor had been a slightly more prominent person in the Oklahoma public mind.

. . .

C. was already there. So were more police cars, ambulances, wreckers, flashing red and blue lights, uniformed officers and tragedy than I had ever seen in my life.

The bridge was actually two bridges twenty yards apart, one for northbound traffic, the other south. Each was two lanes wide and about a mile long. Both were jammed with vehicles and people. As I walked the last hundred yards I saw, off to the right, another cluster of people and cars and lights down the bank of the river. Then I saw the bus. I recognized it immediately as a Silver Eagle, the forty-one-passenger, restroom-equipped pride of the Continental Trailways fleet. Its red-and-cream rear end was sticking out of the muddy water. More than half of the bus was underwater. At least a half-dozen small boats were moving around it. Firemen and frogmen were in the boats and swimming in and around the bus.

C. was in the center of the southbound span. He was

with a group of ten or so other men who were talking and looking down over the rail at the bus and the rescue operation.

He was delighted to see me. He quickly introduced me to the others, who were mostly sheriffs or captains and lieutenants of various kinds. Then he briefed me.

"There were twenty-four people on board, including the driver. We have sixteen bodies out. One guy lived for a while but then drowned. They're pulling the others out as they find them. It's difficult work."

"They've got another," said one of the sheriffs. He and two men stepped aside for me to go to the rail.

There was sudden and absolute silence on the bridge, on the riverbank. As if we were all in church.

The dripping wet body of a white woman in a yellow dress was handed out through a bus window. It was too far away to see how old she was and what she really looked like. Two frogmen gave her to three firemen in a boat. They took her to shore. Another boat came up to the open window. A wet dead man was handed out to them. All I could tell about him was that he was black and that he might have been wearing a light tan suit.

Then, over on the bank, the woman in the yellow dress was laid on a stretcher and covered up with a dark blue blanket.

I heard crying. At the top of the shore was a cluster of maybe seven or eight people. Another of the sheriffs saw me looking. "They're people from around here who say they had relatives on the bus," he said in a soft voice.

There was noise again.

I moved with C. and the other officers farther on toward the middle of the bridge. There was a huge hunk out of the steel rail and girders where the bus had plunged off.

"We have a Texaco tanker driver and a salesman in a car who were right behind the bus," C. said. "They both say it was doing at least fifty, maybe sixty, when it went through there."

"No skid marks," said a sheriff. "No weather problems."

No weather problems was right. It was a November Oklahoma day that was meant to be in a season with a poetic name like "autumn" instead of "fall." The leaves on the trees on both sides of the river were red and yellow and purple like quilts. The sky was like a bedsheet of blue. The sun reflected off the water of the river. A perfect day to be alive in Oklahoma.

Another sheriff said: "It must have been some hit down there against the river and the bottom." He smacked his right fist into his left hand. "Like crashing into a stone wall. Those poor people. Thrown forward on impact. Crushed together, I'll bet, like crickets in a jar."

We drifted away. C. caught my one good eye with both of his. He needed to talk to me privately, was the message. I had received such messages in such ways several times before in our adventures together on behalf of the people and the government of Oklahoma. I patted my coat pockets as if looking for something and said: "I left my pen and notebook back at the car. Want to walk back there with me, C.?"

He said sure, and we both nodded to the sheriffs and walked away.

"We have one very small problem," C. said ever so quietly as we walked, "that needs to be kept very small. Is it an Oklahoma accident or is it a Texas accident? The state line runs right down through the center of the river. The bus was in Oklahoma when it went through the guardrail, but it landed in Texas. Denison is closer than Sturant and it's in Texas and so that's where the bodies are being taken."

"Come on, C.! Who cares?"

We were at my Skylark. I opened the door and faked going through the glove compartment and the sun visors in search of pen and paper.

"Who cares is the Department of Public Safety of both states, the sheriffs of the counties on both sides, and a lot of other people. They care because one or the other is going to get twenty-four more traffic deaths on its record book, just like that. And those stupid statistic things are important to other things."

"Like what, for God's sake?"

"Now you come on, Mack, for *your* God's sake! You know as well as I do all kinds of road money at the federal and state level and traffic-safety awards and jobs and speeches are tied up in those kinds of numbers. Those guys back there are already beginning to sniff around the subject. We could have a real shootout here on the Red River Bridge before it's settled. Daring Dan is on a plane coming this way from the Panhandle, where he was by coincidence just making a speech about traffic safety and the fact that this is the best year for fatalities in the history of Oklahoma since World War Two. I talked to him a while ago on the two-way radio. He wants me to help him get Texas to take the full hit for all twenty-four of these."

Daring Dan was Colonel Dan Burroughs, commander of the Oklahoma Highway Patrol. He was called Daring because he wasn't. C. said he was probably the most cautious man he had ever met in law enforcement. So cautious, he said, that he would close down all highways in the state every time it drizzled, if he had his way. The highway patrol and the OBI were supposed to be partners in the fight against Oklahoma lawlessness, and for the most part they were. That was mainly because C. and Daring Dan negotiated and honored iron-clad turf boundaries, which mostly gave everything difficult and controversial to the OBI and everything easy and mothery to the OHP. And they also agreed to help each other and present a solid front in all skirmishes with the legislature, the executive branch, the public, the press and all others who didn't have the honor and privilege to wear a badge on their chest and carry a gun on their hip.

"There are twenty-four people dead and you people are worrying about traffic awards. . . ."

"Okay, forget it, Mack. If you are not interested in helping out a friend and your state, of which you are the lieutenant governor, then okay."

"You want me to go over and tell the Texans that by

the authority vested in me as lieutenant governor of Oklahoma I hereby assign them this accident and all twenty-four dead people?"

"Something like that."

"I don't have any authority vested in me to do much of anything, C. I can barely get through a police roadblock. Some fourteen-year-old trooper just now not only didn't know who I was, he didn't even seem to know that the state of which he is an employee had a lieutenant governor."

"Did you get his name? I'll get Daring to can him."

"That is not the point. I could go over there and throw my weight around from now to the end of time and it would not mean a thing. That is the point."

"You can be very persuasive. I know of no one in all of Oklahoma and the world who is better at persuading people than you."

"All right, all right. Save the shellac. I'll give it a whirl."

We walked back to the group of sheriffs and captains and lieutenants. I said to them in a voice reserved mostly for funeral eulogies and shopping-mall dedications: "Clearly this is a matter for the State of Oklahoma. I have asked Director Hayes here to take charge of all operations until Colonel Burroughs arrives. They will arrange to have the bodies removed from Denison up to funeral homes in Sturant. They will arrange to meet with the press there to bring the public up-to-date on the accident. . . ."

"Now just a goddamn minute, sir," said one of the Texas sheriffs.

"I assume we're all Christians here, Sheriff," I said. "I am offended by such talk."

He said: "Sorry, sir. I'm a Baptist myself."

"Maybe we should discuss this with our colonel in Austin," said one of the Texas Department of Public Safety captains.

And after a while I became convinced by their arguments that I was wrong. Texas was more entitled to the accident than Oklahoma. So I reversed my position—reluctantly—and, in front of everyone, ordered OBI director Hayes to stand aside but to give Texas all of the Oklahoma assistance it needed in handling this terrible tragedy.

It was one of the most tried-and-true techniques of politics. Buffalo Joe called it Making Mud Pies Look Like Fudge and Then Telling Them They Can't Have Any.

．　．　．

We stayed there at the scene for another hour, until all twenty-four bodies had been retrieved and sent off to Texas and a Denison funeral home in ambulances.

The last body to come out, like a captain last to leave his ship, was that of the driver. C. and I were over on the riverbank when they brought him there in a boat. The Sturant sheriff said he had no idea what the T. in "T. Vermillion" stood for. Everybody in Sturant who knew and loved him called him Buck. Buck Vermillion. And now there he was, dead. He was a tall, trim, handsome man in his late fifties. His dark brown hair was matted down on his head by the water. His eyes were closed. There was no expression on his face. His skin was yellow like that on a freshly dressed chicken. His light gray uniform shirt and his darker gray gabardine trousers were dripping water. So were his black dress shoes. His ticket punch was still in its black leather holster on his right hip. And his black tie was still tied and up tight against the buttoned top button of his shirt.

What happened, Buck Vermillion? What in the world caused your Silver Eagle to go sailing off that bridge?

After a while C. and I left. We headed in my car for Sturant, eighteen miles north, so C. could get in his OBI Cessna for the flight back to Oklahoma City. He had urged me to let a trooper or an OBI agent drive my Skylark to Oklahoma City so I could fly with him. I declined. I had become used to flying on small airplanes, but it was something that I felt should not be overdone. Besides, Jackie, my wife, was out of town at a grocers' convention in Las Vegas, so I had no reason to rush home.

Before leaving Sturant we were also going to pay a call on the widow of the bus driver. The Sturant sheriff asked us to. He gave us her name and address and said we could probably find her either at home or at the bank where she worked and where her friends had gathered, once the word got around about the accident. The sheriff said Buck and Marsha Vermillion were first-class citizens of Sturant. Both of them.

"What do you think happened?" I asked C., as we were driving up Highway 69-75.

"There are only a few possibilities," C. said. "Maybe

Vermillion had a heart attack or a stroke or something like that. Maybe there was a sudden mechanical problem with the bus. The brakes failed and the wheels locked off to the right. That would explain why the witnesses driving behind said they never saw the brake lights come on. Not even as he was going through the guardrail. Or it's always possible some crazy passenger stabbed him in the back or did something else like that. I can't think of anything else. Can you, Mack?"

I shook my head. He had about covered it.

"The Texas people promised to keep me informed," C. said. "Autopsies and mechanical checks and things like that should clear it up pretty fast. Buses don't drive off bridges for no reason."

I changed the subject to Luther. Compared with the bus tragedy, the disappearance of House Speaker Luther Wallace was not very important. But I did have some news and a request. I told him about what I had found at the SSO and what the neighbor woman had said.

"So you have a coincidence," C. said when I was through.

"It's more than that. Call it a Probable Certainty."

"A Probable Certainty that Luther and the SSO man ran off together?"

"It's worth thinking about at least. Why don't you see if there's anything around Luther's house about that Marine reunion? Some other names and addresses. Anything. I am sure Annabel would let you have it. Also, maybe the law enforcement people in Pawnee City might have some word on Thornton of the SSO."

"What happened to the wife?"

"Who knows? Maybe she's out looking for him."

We had arrived at the Sturant Bank and Trust building to talk to the wife of another man who was lost.

. . .

A uniformed guard at the bank door was at first reluctant to let us in. I told him that we had come to see Mrs. Vermillion and that I was the lieutenant governor of Oklahoma and C. here was C., the famous director of the OBI. It was a tough day for impressing people. It was only after C. showed him his badge, his OBI ID card and a few harsh words that we were allowed to enter. The guard, a huge man in his sixties, apologized for his carefulness but reminded us that this was a national bank full of money that was insured and guaranteed by the president of the United States in Washington. He said he had to be careful about all strangers, because bank robbers do not take the day off just because there's been a tragedy at the Red River Bridge. Then he took us through the darkened empty bank lobby to a rear conference room, where he said, "All of 'em are here."

A Mr. Leland Hamilton met us right at the door. Not only did he know who we were, he was impressed with both of us.

"I am with the bank," he said. "Mrs. Vermillion will be so appreciative of your coming by, gentlemen. Thank you."

There are two kinds of bankers. Those who run your life and rub your nose in it, and those who don't. Leland Hamilton struck me as being the second kind. I liked him. On sight. He had wavy black hair and a square face like those actors who play Notre Dame football players in the movies. Both his mouth and his smile were as big as grocery sacks.

He took us directly to Mrs. Vermillion, who was sitting on a leather couch between two other women. She was an attractive person in her late fifties. Trim, well dressed. Together.

"Do you know yet what happened?" she asked almost immediately after introductions.

"No, ma'am," C. said. "There are several possibilities, but nothing has been pinned down as yet."

"Is it true Texas is in charge of the investigation? There was a sheriff's deputy in here a while ago saying Buck would be taken to a funeral home in Denison."

"Yes, ma'am, that's so. The accident technically happened in Texas. But our people are involved, too, and we will make sure it is done right."

"He said they wanted to do an autopsy. Is that necessary?"

"Yes, ma'am, it is. We would have done the same thing if Oklahoma was in charge. It is part of the normal investigation process in accidents like this."

"Buck was not a drinker, if that's what anybody thinks."

"That's not it at all."

There were signs of crying in her blue eyes. It had been a couple of hours now since the accident, though, and that was over.

I expressed to her the sympathy of the governor and the people of Oklahoma for her loss.

"How did you happen to be in the area?" she said.

I told her about the shopping-mall dedication over at Pawnee City.

"We financed several of those stores in that mall," she said. "I hope you dedicated it for a long and healthy haul."

"I did, yes ma'am."

"What is your position on our turnpike?" she asked me. I had forgotten that Sturant was the eastern terminus of one of those stupid things. "The governor, bless his heart, has declared himself. Have you?"

"The governor and I serve Oklahoma together," I said.

"Well, I just hope Speaker Wallace stays gone until it's done," she said. "He's the one who worries me. He'll do anything to stop what he doesn't like. I think we have a chance without him around, don't you?"

"Yes, ma'am."

"What's your stand on our turnpike, Mr. Director?" she said to C.

"The OBI doesn't take stands on turnpikes, Mrs. Vermillion," he said.

He and I shook hands with her again.

"Please keep me posted on the accident investigation," she said.

"Yes, ma'am," we said, almost in unison, like choirboys. I had a feeling right then and there that this woman made all people around her feel like choirboys. And that probably included Buck.

We moved away and toward the door. Leland Hamilton introduced us to the others in the room as we departed. There were two Methodist preachers, a lawyer, three or four women of Mrs. Vermillion's age and two or three people who worked at the bank.

Hamilton, who was probably thirty-five years old, walked us through the lobby toward the front door.

"You are a very young bank president," I said, making conversation.

"Oh, no," he said laughing. "I'm not the president. That's Mrs. Vermillion. It's her bank. I'm the executive vice-president."

C. almost stopped. "She's the president of this bank?"

"That's right."

"How in the hell did she end up married to a bus driver?"

Hamilton lost his smile. He did not like that question. Neither did I.

"I guess it was love, Mr. Hayes," said Hamilton, making me like him even more. "They were high school sweethearts and they married the day they graduated. They have been leading citizens of our town in every respect ever since."

"Sure. Right," C. said, not convinced.

We all three shook hands and the guard let C. and me out.

We were only three steps away from the closed door when I said, "What's this about being married to a bus driver? I have many friends who are bus drivers, and I do not like the implications of that one bit. What if she was married to a cop and I said, 'How in the hell did she end up married to a cop?'"

"Okay, okay, you're right. Please accept my apology on behalf of all of the bus drivers of the world. But Mack, you will have to admit it is unusual to have a woman president of a bank. And even more unusual to have one who is married to a bus driver."

"So it's unusual?"

"So that's all I'm saying. It's unusual."

3
· · ·
BRAKE LIGHTS

B Y LUNCH the next day, C. had what we needed on the Luther business. It was a Xerox copy of a two-page letter of invitation to the Marine officers' reunion in Kansas City. It was to all "Sukiran Irregulars," whatever that meant, and was written in a kind of military-jargon garble. Probably as a joke. But the important thing was that it listed names, with addresses and phone numbers, of fourteen people "Ordered to Muster to Drink, Be Merry and Lie" in Kansas City on September 6, a month and a day before Luther disappeared. Luther and Thornton were two of the fourteen.

We were, as usual, in the backseat of C.'s cruising car. We had gone through the drive-thru at Pizza Heaven #5 on 63rd. C. had his usual. I had a green-pepper-and-onion.

"Okay, now what?" C. asked.

"Now we call these others."

"And ask them what?"

"If they know anything about where Luther may have run off to."

"I can't do that. No laws have been broken. Some idiot lawyer would hang me out to dry. I told Annabel Wallace we were still on the case informally, but I can't do much more. . . ."

I folded the letter up and put it in my suitcoat pocket. "I'll take care of it."

"Be careful. You never know when you're going to turn up a hornet's nest."

"Thank you, sir."

"You are welcome, sir."

I asked him what, if anything, he had found out from the police in Pawnee City.

"Nothing, really. Thornton's wife, whose name is Sarah, by the way, came by the police station two or so weeks ago and asked if they had picked up any information about her husband. It was a strange kind of thing, they said. She finally told them he had been missing and while she was sure nothing was wrong she just thought she would check. They asked if she wanted to file a Missing Persons on him. No, she said. Their guess is that it was a sex deal. That Thornton ran off with another woman. I asked them why they guessed that and the guy said that was what they always guessed in deals like that. No other reason. I asked about where Mrs. Thornton got off to. They have no idea. They didn't even know she was gone."

We drifted on to the Turnpike Shootout. C. wanted to know if Buffalo Joe really was going to push for those two things when the legislature convened in January. I told him as far as I could tell, yes. Particularly with Luther out of the picture.

"I'll bet he'll name them for himself," C. said. "That's it! I'll bet that's the whole story here. Right. That is it. Can't you see it? Driving up to a toll gate and seeing a huge sign, 'The Buffalo Chip Memorial Turnpike,' with his picture all engraved in marble right over where you toss two quarters in a basket. The name. That is the important thing still to come out. I'll bet you anything it has to do with the names of those stupid turnpikes."

Neither of us knew at the time how close to the truth that was going to turn out to be.

But I didn't want to talk about the turnpikes. We were almost back at the capitol and I wanted to know if there was anything new on the Red River bus thing.

C. said: "The autopsy on Vermillion turned up nothing. He was in perfect health. Death was from the crash. No heart attack, no stroke, nothing like that. Also, no gunshots or knife stabs in the back or anywhere else. In other words, Mack, that man was sitting up there behind the wheel of that bus fully alert and alive to what was going on when it sailed off the bridge."

"Wow. What an awful thought."

"It only leaves the mechanics. They've taken the bus down to the Trailways main garage in Dallas for a full going over. We'll see. I understand there are insurance people crawling over the case now, too, of course."

"Heard any more about the Vermillions?"

"No. Didn't expect to. What are you getting at?"

"Oh, I just thought there might be a reason to see what their life and all that was like there in Sturant."

"Oh, now, wait a minute, Mr. Lieutenant Governor. I surely hope you are not suggesting there is something strange about a woman bank president being married to a bus driver."

"I just can't get it out of my mind. Like you said, it *is* unusual, that's all."

"All right. I'll have our district agent down there see what he can put together."

"As coincidence would have it, I have to go to Dallas the day after tomorrow for an Association of State Legislatures regional workshop on water policy. Maybe I'll stop by the Trailways garage. I have always wanted to see it."

. . .

The first three calls drew blanks. Two of them had not gone to Kansas City. The third, a retired career Marine officer in San Diego, was clearly much older than Luther and Thornton. He said he had gone to the reunion but nothing had happened that he could remember, and could I please call him back sometime next week because he was on his way out the door to play at a 1st Marine Division Seniors golf tournament up at a Marine base called Pendleton. I knew about Pendleton. Pepper had gone there right out of boot camp before he was sent to Korea to die.

Call four was paydirt. It was to Jonas Jensen, the man in Kansas City whose name was on the invitation letter. His business phone number was at the *Kansas City Star,* a newspaper. I asked for Jensen and was connected to a man who identified himself as Mark Wrobel, the deputy executive editor, and asked if he could help me. I told him I wished to talk to Jensen.

"He's gone for now," said the voice of Mark Wrobel. "Gone from the newspaper."

"How long's he been gone?"

"Since October."

"Did he up and leave suddenly?"

"Sir, if you have any other questions, I suggest you contact Detective Sergeant McAlpin with the Kansas City Police. He is in charge of the investigation."

• • •

C. had a friend in the Missouri State Police who cleared the way for me to get the full story from Detective Sergeant McAlpin. McAlpin said Jonas Jensen did not show up for work one morning. He had worked at the *Star* for fifteen years, having come there from a smaller paper in a smaller city in Illinois. He had been an assistant managing editor for eight years. The people at the *Star* had filed a Missing Persons after the third day and after there was no answer at the phone or door of his apartment, south of downtown Kansas City. He was divorced and lived alone, and apparently nobody else had missed him enough to do anything about it. As in Luther's case, the police had checked every conceivable foul-play possibility but finally put the case file away as a probable noncriminal matter.

"My best guess is he just decided to go away for a while without telling anybody," McAlpin said. "Who wouldn't want to do that, is what I say. What about you, Mr. Lieutenant Governor? I can't think of anything better than one day driving to work and to just keep driving. Say nothing to nobody. Not my wife, not my kids, not my captain, not my nobody. Just keep driving. Instead of taking the downtown exit off the Southwest Freeway, just keep going. Through Emporia and Wichita and the rest of Kansas to New Mexico and Arizona and the mountains and deserts and Nevada and maybe to California. Or maybe just stop along the way anywhere and stay forever. Everybody wants to do that, Mr. Lieutenant Governor. Everybody. That's probably all Jensen has done. And what I say is, More power to him. Haven't you ever been tempted to do the same thing? Driving into work there in Oklahoma as lieutenant governor and saying, To hell with this, I am running away. Sure you have. That's what this is all about. Unless he's been murdered or something. That's always possible. He was not queer or on drugs, by the way. And he had a clean nose. Clean all the way. Didn't even screw prostitutes. None of the regulars, at least. We checked them. So there you are, sir."

So there you are, sir.

McAlpin had only one clue as to where Jensen might have gone. "His ex-wife said he loved France, which sounds crazy from everything I've heard about France. It made him think he was Ernest Hemingway. You know, the dead writer. He blew his brains out a while ago somewhere out west."

Yeah. I had read a couple of his short stories in junior college. And I must say I had loved them. Particularly one about two killers coming to get a guy at a diner. I had also read *The Old Man and the Sea,* which was a novel that had been published first in *Life* magazine. It was about an old Cuban fisherman going after the biggest fish of all. By the time it was over, my hands felt like they were bleeding and the rest of my body was hurting just like the old man's. Hemingway was some writer. He wrote mostly in short sentences that were easy to understand.

I got Jensen's ex-wife's name and number from McAlpin and said good-bye.

But before I could dial the number, my secretary, Janice Alice Montgomery, broke in on the intercom line to say a crying woman was on hold. She said the woman said she was the wife of Bob Thornton, the manager of the SSO in Pawnee City.

"He's vanished, Mr. Lieutenant Governor," said the woman the second after I said hello. "I think he's run off someplace with Luther Wallace, the speaker. My sister later figured out that it was you who came in the store the other day. She saw your picture on the TV down at the Red River Bridge bus thing. Luther called him right there in the store the day before they both disappeared. I answered the phone. I know it was Luther. He didn't say it was him, but I know it was. I've been off at my sister's house. I didn't want to have to say anything to anybody when they asked about where Bob was. A couple of SSO people came in today. They demanded my sister tell them where Bobby was. They are threatening to close us down. What is going on, Mr. Lieutenant Governor?"

She cried for a few seconds. Then I said, "Did your husband ever say anything about France or a writer named Hemingway?"

"No, sir," she said. "He only had a little Spanish and that was almost gone."

. . .

The Dallas symposium was on the Ogallala Aquifer crisis. The crisis was that in twenty to forty years we of the Great Plains—Oklahoma, Kansas, New Mexico, Colorado, Nebraska and Texas—were going to be without water, which by then would have become as precious a commodity as oil and gas. The Ogallala Aquifer was a natural underground water reservoir that had been providing all of us water, and now it was drying up as a result of rampant abuse and overuse by us all. There were geologists and waterists and experts of all kinds with dire predictions. There were also scads of expensive solutions thrown out for discussion, the most absurd being the notion that we were all going to end up relying on Arkansas for our water supply. One guy had an elaborate set of charts and slides that showed Arkansas with enough water in its rivers and streams to supply all of Texas, Oklahoma and Kansas for the next five hundred years. The only problem was getting it from there to here. The proposed solution was to dig a gigantic ditch from Arkansas to all of the other states and thus make us forever dependent on Arkansas for our very lives. The whole thing sounded stupid and very far away. And mostly boring. The only interesting part was some University of Nebraska professor's presentation of an elaborate security plan to protect the ditches from sabotage. It included highly sophisticated sensors on fences and around-the-clock dog and helicopter and laser-equipped watchtower surveillance. The professor said the Romans had lost their empire partly because they had failed to protect their viaducts from the enemy. Nobody ever asked who might be the enemy of the new Great Arkansas Viaduct System, or GAVS, as it was called by the professor and the other proponents. Ridiculous.

I was delighted to have the Continental Trailways garage to slip away to. It was a magnificent facility just west of downtown Dallas on the other side of an eight-lane freeway named after somebody named Stemmons. It sounded familiar to me and after a while I remembered that it was the one the presidential motorcade had traveled on to the hospital after President Kennedy had been shot.

The Red River Silver Eagle was in a back corner of the garage, which was filled with red-and-white Silver and Golden Eagles, GMs and other buses in various stages of undress and disrepair. There must have been at least twenty buses on racks or with their motors out or something. Another sixty or seventy were parked outside on a gigantic lot, mostly waiting their turn to go out on runs or for servicing rather than for repair work. A little bit of heaven, in other words, for somebody like me who admired and appreciated buses. Like Fred Rayburn's bus museum.

The Red River bus was behind yellow ropes that had little "Police Evidence—Keep Out" signs on them. C. had cleared it with the Texas Department of Public Safety for me to get in to see it and I had done some clearing of my own. I had had my friend, the manager of the Oklahoma City bus depot, Hugh B. Glisan, make a call or two to Dallas on my behalf. So Trailways had known I was coming and they had assigned their vice-president for operations and safety to escort me around. His name was Brown, Dean Brown. He was a tall, heavy man and was extremely emotional about what had happened.

"It makes me cry every time I see it," he said on our way back to the bus. "I hear the panicked voices of those dying passengers, I imagine doomed Buck Vermillion struggling to keep his bus on the road and his precious human cargo alive."

It was indeed an awful sight. The first third of the bus was crushed like a toy bus some kid had beaten in with a hammer. The front door through which those twenty-four people had entered was mashed up in there somewhere with metal and the windshield and the destination sign and the headlights. And the driver's seat. The sheriff on the bridge had been right. The bus had hit the water and the river bottom with a terrific force. The muddy water of the river had left a mark across the side of the bus at an upward angle from the front, and had left much of the top and all of the rear clean and glistening. It was like somebody had painted the front section with a brush of red mud. The six-foot-long silver eagle emblem was completely covered. It was only up close that I could clearly make out the screaming eagle head and the red, white and blue streamers flowing out of its mouth through a circle that said "Silver Eagle."

"Look at him," said Dean Brown of the eagle emblem. "He's crying for those poor helpless souls inside." His eyes had teared up.

My eyes did the same thing when I stood on one of the two stepladders that had been placed along the side of the bus. The huge windows had all been pushed open. I climbed up and peered inside. Most of the forty-one reclining seats were still fastened to the floor. The front ones were coated with red mud. Those in back were clean and fresh, except for the rips in some of them. Had the passengers grabbed them so ferociously they had torn the fabric? Had those in back tried frantically to keep from being thrown forward? It was like looking into a horrible death chamber. Twenty-four people died inside this space I was now looking into like a peeping tom on a ladder.

It wasn't much consolation to think so, but thank God there were only twenty-four passengers instead of a full load of forty-one.

Dean Brown, on the other ladder, and I were completely still. It was like the silence on the bridge whenever a body had been taken out of the bus.

Several minutes later we were both back down on the

concrete floor of the garage, and I asked Dean Brown a few questions, the very few I had come to ask.

"Has anything turned up yet on the mechanical condition of the bus at the time of the accident?" I said.

"We have just begun the detail work," he said. "Are you asking unofficially and prematurely?"

"I am."

He gave me a professional's report: "Well. The steering column appears to have been damaged only in the crash. Best we can tell, it was working fine and was not locked or anything like that. The brakes? So far, it appears they were fine. This bus was only eighteen months old. It rolled off the assembly line in our Harlingen plant last spring. It was on a regular scheduled maintenance program. All safety and basic systems were thoroughly checked just three months ago. The tires were almost new. Ninety-eight-percent treads. In other words, sir, so far it appears whatever happened was not the bus's fault. But please keep in mind that we have not yet done the detailed X-ray and other work that the DPS and the insurance companies and everybody else are going to want to do. Right now it's only us bus people who have done the work."

"What about the brake lights? Were they working?"

"Somebody may have checked that, but I don't know the result. It's all so torn up there at the driver's seat, they were most likely surely disconnected in the accident—but let me see."

Then Dean Brown did what I could not have done.

He climbed back on one of the ladders and swung a leg over and through one of the open windows. And disappeared.

In a few seconds he yelled, "I found the brake pedals. Go around to the back and see what you can see."

I walked to the rear of the bus, which was in perfect condition.

"Here goes!" Dean Brown yelled.

Both of the huge red brake lights blinked on.

It was amazing they still worked.

So if doomed Buck Vermillion was struggling to save his bus and his precious human cargo, he was doing so without doing what most people would do by reflex when something they were driving was headed off a bridge: put on the brakes.

.   .   .

"However you cut it, you are saying Buck Vermillion drove that bus off that bridge deliberately," C. said. "And that is one lunatic theory. It's one thing to commit suicide, it's another to take twenty-three innocent people with you when you do it. This man would not have done that."

I replied: "I have said nothing about suicide. I have said only that it is pretty sure now that he did not put the brakes on. Something crazy was going on in that bus. It doesn't have to be suicide to be crazy."

"Well, everything our people turned up about him is anything but crazy. He was Mr. Wonderful. Deacon in the church, scoutmaster, volunteer father for orphans, you name it. Mr. Perfect Citizen. Very much a second fiddle to his important wife, a little on the dumb side, apparently . . ."

He looked at me sheepishly.

"But for a bus driver what can you expect? Right?" I said.

"Mrs. Vermillion's maiden name was Sturant. The town was named after a great-great-uncle of some kind. She inherited that bank."

"Must have made for an interesting life for Buck Vermillion," I said.

C. grabbed my right hand and started shaking it. "Call me when you get there," he said.

It was 8:10 two mornings after my late-evening return from Dallas. We were at a Braniff boarding gate at Will Rogers Airport in Oklahoma City, where C. had driven me because Jackie was still in Las Vegas. My plane had just been called.

"Take it easy on the pizza while I'm gone," I said.

"Sure thing. And you lay off those fries those Frenchmen are so famous for," he replied.

He said that because I was off to France in search of Luther Wallace.

4
. . .
LIBERTÉ

I T WAS my first trip to France, Europe and over-seas. It was the first time I had come as close to New York City as its airport named after President Kennedy and the first time I had flown on one of those huge 747 jetliners. I went on Braniff 707s from Oklahoma City to Kansas City and then nonstop to Kennedy Airport. I had a middle seat all the way. On the fifty-five-minute Kansas City leg a fat white man in coveralls sat on my left and a thin black woman on my right. Neither said a word to me or to anyone else. The woman read a *U.S. News & World Report* she had gotten from a stewardess. The man read some paperback book he had brought with him. He smelled like shoe polish and toothpaste. She smelled like perfume. I read nothing. I just closed my eyes and wondered what the whole trip was going to be like. And thought about Buck Vermillion.

There were three stewardesses on duty. Two blondes and a brunette. All were young and pretty and showoffs. They walked up and down the aisle aware and happy that all of the men in aisle seats were staring at their legs and bottoms. Like at a strip show in one of those places on Sheridan in Oklahoma City. I have never been to one, but I knew enough to know what they were like.

They served us coffee, a choice of juices, and a cheese Danish wrapped in cellophane.

I wondered how long it would be before Nita Pickens of Perkins Corner or some other world-famous country music star wrote a song about Buck and his twenty-three passengers scrambling and screaming for their lives as that bus sailed off the Red River Bridge. I had met Nita Pickens, one of Oklahoma's most famous citizens, at a college commencement a few years back. I had been the commencement speaker and she had gotten the Distinguished Alumnus Award. My speech had inspired her to write "Risk It, O Baby of Mine," which was not as big a seller as her two major all-times, "Hugotown Hug" and "I Lost My Heart at Walgreen's and Walked on over to Sears," but it was number one on the C&W charts for more than six weeks. That may not sound like that big a deal, but on the other hand how many people have lived their lives *without* ever inspiring a number-one C&W song? I'll bet that Trooper Kid back at the bridge would have been impressed. That's what I'll do next time. Instead of saying I am the lieutenant governor of Oklahoma, I'll say I am the man who made the speech that caused Nita Pickens of Perkins Corner to write "Risk It, O Baby of Mine."

... Maybe there had been somebody with a gun on that bus. Maybe the gunman forced Buck Vermillion to drive off the bridge. But why? If the gunman wanted to kill himself, all he had to do was put the gun to his own head. Unless he was a real lunatic, why kill all of those other people, too? Maybe he was threatening to do harm to someone else on the bus? What if Buck got into some kind of diversionary or chicken game with the gunman and lost control of the bus? Why, then, didn't he put on the brakes? Always it came back to: Why didn't he put on the brakes? Maybe he couldn't put on the brakes. Maybe he was asleep. Asleep. Yeah. That's it! A simple and understandable explanation. Why in the hell had I not thought of that before? Sure, it was in the broad daylight of the afternoon, but people doze off then, too. How many times had Buck driven that route? Hundreds, thousands, millions? He was bored for sure. Bored enough to doze off for the few seconds it would take that bus to swerve out of control and over the bridge. But wait a minute. Some of the passengers must have seen what was happening. Wouldn't at least one of them have yelled out? *Hey, driver! We're going off the bridge!* Wouldn't that have roused Buck enough at least to cause the normal human reflex of slamming down on the brake pedal? There must have also been a terrific noise from crashing through the rail.

My thinking ended with the terrible possibility that we might never know for sure what happened. That would be truly awful. I like to know things like that. So did C.

We were on the ground in Kansas City for almost an hour, but I did not get off. I could have if I had taken my boarding pass with me so I could reboard with the Kansas City passengers.

Mrs. Hegner, a blue-haired widow lady from Garden City, Kansas, replaced the fat man on the aisle. She sat down talking a streak that was as blue as her hair. She said she had flown into Kansas City on a tiny Kansas Air commuter with only ten seats. She said this was her fourth trip to New York on a plane, which was a surprise. Her oldest daughter was married to a radio announcer in Trenton, New Jersey, and they had three children. A boy, who was named William T. after his late grandfather, her husband; and two girls who spent most of their time listening to filthy records you couldn't even buy in Kansas.

They served us our choice of cold drinks free. Cocktails, wine and beer were also available to buy, but since I do not drink alcohol I had a Pepsi. Mrs. Hegner from Garden City had a vodka martini, which was a surprise. She asked me what I did for a living and I told her. But I do not think she believed I was the lieutenant governor of Oklahoma. Particularly after I told her I was actually born and had grown up in Medicine Bend, Kansas. Don't you have to be native-born to be a lieutenant governor or governor of a state? she said. From the second she sat down I knew she wanted to know about the left eye. Everybody did. Finally, just after they told us to fasten our seat belts for the landing at New York City, she finally asked. I told her the truth: I had been hit in the face by a kicked can in a kick-the-can game. She was stunned and delighted. She said she had always warned her own children about just such a possible horror when they had played that game, but she had never heard of it actually happening.

I had to wait three and a half hours to ride a yellow shuttle bus from the Braniff terminal around to another to catch the big Pan Am to Nice, France. "Nice" is pronounced "neese." That 747 was one huge machine. So huge, frankly, it was difficult for me to understand how it could get off the ground and actually fly. It carried at least three hundred passengers, seated eleven across in a three/five/three-in-a-row arrangement. I had a window seat halfway back in the section, which was fine with me. We took off about forty minutes late, and the pilot said it was because a warning light of some kind had come on by mistake but they did not want to take any chances. . . .

Stop. No more. Not about the flight over. Nor any other flight. It is too much like Fred L. Hoover. Fred was a regional credit executive for Western Auto who lived on our block in Oklahoma City. He made his weekly rounds of the small cities of Oklahoma, Kansas, Missouri, Texas, Arkansas and New Mexico by airliner, and Friday night he'd come home and tell anybody who would listen about every flight he had been on that week. He described each landing and takeoff, each meal, each complimentary beverage, each pilot's chat to the passengers, each patch of clear-air turbulence, each arrival and departure time.

It was his life, and he thought it was a most exciting life that should be shared with his friends and neighbors. The worst part of it was the way he compared his flights. It was bumpy going into Albuquerque on Trans Texas flight 533 the other night, but it was nothing like the bumpiness on that Continental flight to Lubbock two weeks ago. The food was bad going to Houston, but worse going to Corpus Christi. Fred L. Hoover had total recall for every detail of every flight he had ever taken.

The only really important thing about my flight to Nice was my mission. I was on my way to see if I could talk Luther into coming back home to Oklahoma. Annabel had asked me to give it a try on her behalf and at her expense. If I wanted to. If I was that interested. Clearly, she could take it or leave it. C. and I were certain that if I had said no, it was unlikely she would have asked anyone else to make the trip.

We had gone to her with the news that Luther had been found. Jonas Jensen's ex-wife had given me the name of the French town she would bet anything he had gone to. It was called La Napoule, which in French meant "the worm." Through an FBI friend, C. had gotten the French police to check it out. Yes, indeed. Luther, Jensen, Thornton and two other American men in their forties were living there in the Hôtel La Liberté.

The FBI agent told C. *liberté* was French for "freedom."

· · ·

I decided to call C. from a pay phone at the Nice airport. A female operator who spoke English with a very heavy

accent came on like the people who worked in the gift
shops and other places I had gone into while waiting at
Kennedy. She acted like it was a terrible imposition to do
her job by putting through a call to a C. Harry Hayes in
Oklahoma City, Oklahoma, USA. It's probably not fair
and I do not know how it got started, but in southeastern
Oklahoma she would have been accused of having New
Jersey Manners.

C. answered the phone on the second ring. He sounded
a bit drowsy. But otherwise the connection was remarkably clear. I had expected there to be static and other
problems. The only thing was that we couldn't both speak
at the same time. It was like talking on two-way radios.

"Well, I'm here," I said.

"Great," he said. "What did Luther say about what
he's done?"

"I haven't talked to him yet. I'm still at the airport."

"What's up, then?"

"Nothing. You told me to give you a ring when I got
here."

"Hey, Mack, what time is it there?"

I looked up at a clock on a wall. "Eight-fifteen in the
morning."

"You know what time that makes it here? It makes it
one-fifteen in the morning. There's a seven-hour time
difference, Mack."

"I know that. So what?"

"So I was sound asleep. So call me when you talk to
Luther and you know something."

"Do *you* know anything?"

"No, not really. Except that some sickie sent an anonymous note to Mrs. Vermillion, Buck's widow. It said Buck murdered those people. Said he was a premeditated killer."

"See?"

"See what?"

"See how strange it all is."

"Mack, there are sick people out there who prey on people involved in tragedies. It happens so often it's almost normal. It's absurd to think Buck Vermillion, who as far as we can tell had never in his life done a thing wrong or even fishy, would suddenly decide to commit suicide and mass murder. Forget it, Mack. Nothing is that strange. Maybe there in France but not in Oklahoma. Those French people are affecting your mind already."

"The only Frenchman I've talked to already is a woman telephone operator with New Jersey Manners."

"I'm going back to sleep. Call me when you know something about Luther."

"Are you going to check out the letter?"

"We're running it for fingerprints and all the rest. But I'd bet anything there's nothing to it. I shouldn't have even mentioned it. You put all of this out of your mind and concentrate on bringing Luther Wallace back to his senses."

"What about the possibility that Buck Vermillion just fell asleep at the wheel? Regular people do that all the time, too. Would there be something in the autopsy about that?"

C. waited two beats before answering. And when he did, his voice was a quiet, normal C. voice.

"Mr. One-Eyed Mack, I think once again you have shown that under that unassuming, modest one-eyed lieutenant-governor way of yours pulsates a mind of starlike brilliance."

"Are you pulsating a smile or are you serious?"

"Both. No autopsy will show whether he was dozing off. But it sure adds up."

"Except for one thing. The brake lights. No matter how asleep he was, there's no way he wouldn't have roused enough to slam those brakes on as he was going over."

"You are still hung up on those lights, aren't you? Call me with a Luther report."

"Yes sir, Mr. Unassuming Modest One-Eared C."

• • •

I rented a car and drove straight to La Napoule. On with the job of Finding Luther. The Avis car woman, who was young and tanned like an old leather shoe, drew the ten-mile route to La Napoule on a small one-sheet Avis map. I had expected the driving to be different and difficult. It wasn't.

There was a freeway all the way that reminded me a lot of I-40 coming into El Reno. Nothing Frenchy or foreign-special, in other words.

I had given much, much thought to how Luther might react to seeing me. I had visualized everything. From a quiet, routine Well, hi there, Mack, welcome to France, to an emotional, screaming Leave me alone, Mack! Get out of here! I had even considered the possibility of violence: he and his Marine friends might decide to take me prisoner.

The man at the front desk of the Hôtel La Liberté told me to look for the Americans at a restaurant down the street. He pronounced "Americans" so the "cans" came out "cains."

I found them sitting under a tree in the garden part of the restaurant, which was an elaborate white stucco place that must have been a mansion before it was a restaurant. It was almost three in the afternoon, but Luther and his buddies were still eating lunch. Or what remained of it.

Luther saw me almost the second I stepped out the back door of the restaurant and started for him. He jumped to his feet. His face jumped into a joyous smile.

"My God, it's The One-Eyed Mack! Halle-sweet-lujah!"

Halle-sweet-lujah? Luther was already a different man.

He was also wearing white pants, sandals with no socks, a pink short-sleeved shirt unbuttoned down to his navel. He had a beard, which he had never had before. He wore rimless sunglasses, which he had never had before. There was the color of sun and ease on his face which he also had never had before.

He grabbed my right hand with both of his. "Mack, Mack, The One-Eyed Mack. *Bonjour,* Mr. Lieutenant Governor. Welcome to France."

The four others had stayed in their seats. Luther introduced them one at a time. Somebody named Preacher Hancock. Somebody named Reg Runyan. The newspaperman from Kansas City, Jonas Jensen. And somebody named Bob Thornton, manager of a Sooner State Optical store in Pawnee City, Oklahoma. He was balding and fat. His hair was thin. His stomach was a bubble. It was hard to imagine him a Marine officer like Luther. Bob Thornton, no offense, looked not like what he had been but like what he had become. The manager of an SSO in Pawnee City, Oklahoma. He stood and took my hand.

"Fancy meeting you here, Mr. Lieutenant Governor," Bob Thornton said, like it was a joke and he was the funniest SSO man in Oklahoma. "Do you bring news from where the wind comes sweeping down the plain?"

"Yes, indeed," I said. "Your wife is worried to death about you."

He did not change his pleasant expression. He gave me a smart salute, sat back down and took another swallow of whatever there was in the glass in front of him.

Jonas Jensen looked just as I had imagined. Red-faced, broad, huge, Hemingway. Like Luther, believable at a glance as an ex–Marine officer. The other two, Hancock and Runyan, could have been anything. They, like Luther, Thornton and Jensen, had beards and grins.

"Jonas here was right in the middle of a story," the one named Runyan said to me. "It's about his duties as VD Control officer."

I sat down and Jonas Jensen, the man with the red face, continued his story without a word of explanation to me.

Luther and the others offered none, either. But it was not hard to follow. Jensen had an actor's voice that was as large as he was.

"So the colonel said to me: 'I have just been notified that our battalion has the highest VD rate in the regiment. As we speak, Lieutenant, twenty-seven percent of our men, of all enlisted ranks from sergeant major to private, are infected. The mathematicians in this outfit can tell you what the numbers add up to. Twenty-seven percent means that exactly two percent more than one out of every four of our Marines is crippled. Two percent more than one out of every four of our Marines would meet the enemy at less than fighting strength. That means, Lieutenant, that if we were called upon to fight the communists we would do so with a force with its combat-effectiveness seriously impaired by clap and crabs. Like fighting with at least one hand tied behind us. The United States of America, the United States Marine Corps, the Third Marine Division, our regiment, this battalion and my ass cannot tolerate this situation. As VD Control officer, Lieutenant, your assignment is to conceptualize a plan that will immediately reduce our VD rate and then to execute that plan. I anticipate your being highly successful, because I hereby alert you to the fact that if my ass and my career goes down over this, yours goes with me.'"

Luther caught my good eye. To Jensen, he said, "I've heard the story, Jonas. Maybe my friend Mack here and I might take a walk, if your feelings won't be too hurt."

Jensen smiled and waved us away. He could not have cared less.

I followed Luther back up through the restaurant and onto the narrow, crowded, noisy brick streets of La Napoule.

"Is that a true story? Did twenty-seven percent of those Marines really have venereal disease?" I asked Luther the second we were outside.

"True story all the way."

"How did they catch it?"

Luther looked over at me, shook his head and said: "From sexual intercourse, Mack. They got it from having sexual intercourse with members of the opposite sex who were infected with same."

"Thank you, sir, for that fact sheet. I know *that*. Where did all of this happen?"

"Okinawa. Where we all were together many years ago."

After a few more steps in silence, he said:

"Annabel send you?"

"That's right."

"Is she okay?"

"She's fine."

"I knew she'd be fine. Finer without me than with me, in fact."

We were down by some water, where hundreds of boats were tied up. They ranged from tiny little sailboats to huge yachts fit for kings and queens.

"She wants you to come home, Luther," I said.

"I do not believe you."

"She sent me here to ask you to. She's paying all of my expenses for this trip. . . ."

"Technically, I am paying for your trip, Mack. All of her money came from me." He slapped me on the back and laughed. "Think about it. I am paying for you to come to France to try and talk me out of doing something I am enjoying very much. Think about it, Mack."

"The legislature and the people of Oklahoma need you."

"Oh, Mack, we don't have to play-act anymore. You know and I know that nobody really needs people like you and me. Give it another week or two and I'll bet you money there won't be two people outside my family who will remember who I was and what I even looked like. People like you and me are grains of sand. We're pretty there on the public beach for a while, and then along comes a puff of wind and we're gone. Puff, gone. Gone. Puff. Who was that guy who used to be speaker? Lucas or Luther something, wasn't it? Didn't he murder his mother or turn Catholic? Puff. Gone. Puff, puff. Gone."

"Well, if nothing else, we need you to stop Joe from building those silly turnpikes."

Luther let out a whoop that Joe probably could have heard back in Oklahoma if he had been listening. He threw his hands up over his head and looked out across the water toward the horizon. "Thank you, God of us all, for delivering me forever from silly turnpikes." He said it like he was praying at an outdoor revival.

We walked onto a concrete embankment on one side of the harbor. We sat down on it and dangled our feet over the water of what Luther said was the Mediterranean Sea, some twenty feet below us.

"Why did you run away, Luther?" I said.

"Because I was up to here with being responsible."

"Responsible for what?"

"Not responsible for *what*. I mean responsible. Being a responsible son, husband, father, friend, attorney, legislator, speaker. I mean being responsible all day, every day of my life. I have been responsible since my father told me to be responsible. The first words he spoke to me and the last words he spoke to me: Be a responsible man and citizen, Luther. Do the right thing, he said, and you will never have a thing to worry about. I have always done the right thing, Mack. Always. Always responsible. Always behaved. Always the good boy. Always, always. Except for one brief period of my life."

"The Marines?"

"That's right."

"So all this is about being a bad boy again?"

Luther seemed to draw back and take a breath. Then he said, "There's a common awful word that common awful people say for 'sexual intercourse,' that thing we were talking about a minute ago. You may even be vaguely familiar with it, Mack. It begins with the letter *f*."

"What's your point, Luther?"

"Well, say that word to yourself. Put 'you' after it and you have my response to what you just said."

In the nearly fourteen years I had known and worked around Luther Wallace in the government of Oklahoma, it was the first time I had ever heard him even come close to using a cuss word. It was one of the things that had drawn us together as friends. I did not cuss, either.

But here he was. In France. A runaway. Using—almost using, at least—the cuss word that began with *f.* The worst one.

5

· · ·

GO-GAAH

I WAS GIVEN a room at the La Liberté that did not have its own commode or shower. They were down the hall in a bathroom I had to share with several other guests. All my room had was a washbasin and something called a *bidet,* pronounced "bih-*day.*" It looked like a commode without anything to sit on. I asked the bellboy what it was for and he said, "You Americains would say 'to wash up after f——.' " Clearly, France was everything I had heard it was.

And as C. had said on the phone, France was also on another clock from Oklahoma's. It was nearly five in the evening in La Napoule when Luther and I got to the hotel, where we had walked in silence after our talk on the embankment. There was a seven-hour difference, so that meant it was almost ten in the morning back in

Oklahoma City. With the exception of maybe an hour-and-a-half catnap on the plane, I had had no sleep the night before, and here it was already early the next evening.

Luther agreed that maybe we could pick up our conversation after I got some rest. He said he and his friends were going to an exhibition at an art museum that evening and I was welcome to join them. What kind of art? I asked. French, he replied. What kind of French? Paul Gauguin French. He pronounced "Gauguin" like it was spelled "Go-gaah." I had never heard of Paul Go-gaah.

My hotel room was unlike anything I had ever slept in before. The bedspread and the wallpaper and the curtains and the towels were all of the same color and design. Big red roses printed on a soft Lava-soap white. I took off my clothes and got under the covers and was asleep in a few minutes.

It was dark and scary when I woke up three hours later. It took a few seconds for me to remember where I was and why I was there. To remember that I did not have my own bathroom. To remember that I was in a place where the rooms were equipped with special equipment for sexual intercourse, where the bellhops used the coarsest words in the language. To remember that Annabel Wallace was paying my way to see if I could talk her husband into returning to Oklahoma. To remember the grins on the faces of that husband and his four friends.

I took a shower down the hall and dressed as casually as I could. I had brought no sports clothes, so it meant wearing a white dress shirt with no tie and the pants from my dark blue year-round–weight suit. That suit, which I had worn on the plane, and four shirts and four changes of underwear were all I had brought with me. Jackie had urged me to throw in a pair of jeans and a couple of pullover knit shirts but I'd declined. Now I very much wished I had followed her advice.

It was after nine o'clock by the time I got down to the lobby. The foulmouthed bellhop was still on duty. He pointed me toward the art museum with the Go-gaah exhibition.

. . .

I had never set foot inside a real art museum or gallery except places with western art, like the National Cowboy Hall of Fame, until I was thirty-seven years old. And even then it had happened only in my line of duty as lieutenant governor. A traveling exhibition of French paintings had come to the Oklahoma City Art Museum, and the museum had held a big black-tie preview dinner to raise money for its children's art education program. Governor Hayman was supposed to represent the highest levels of our state government at the dinner, but at the last minute he backed out and asked me to substitute for him. The chairman of the art museum board that year was a Republican banker who made the mistake of acting like one. A week before the museum affair he'd signed a fund-raising letter for a nonpartisan organization called Oklahomans for Clean Government, which had been set up to recruit clean candidates for statewide office. Like governor. Joe believed in only one kind of politics: partisan.

At any rate, I had been taken with a lot of the pictures I'd seen that night. They were by French artists called Impressionists. Neither Jackie nor I knew what an Impressionist was, and because everybody else there seemed to, we never asked. But the paintings were full of color and light and life and fun, even those that made no sense because the people's faces and bodies or the buildings and trees or whatever was blurred and unrecognizable. Some of them even looked as if the artists had gotten tired before they finished. And I also thought there might have been a little too much nudity for our Oklahoma young and Baptists who might go to the museum. But I kept quiet about it. I figured it was hard enough to rouse support for culture without some one-eyed politician who didn't know an Impressionist from an SSO manager causing trouble over a few exposed breasts and crotches. My favorites were paintings of ballerinas and people sitting in cafés by a guy named Degas, pronounced "day-*gah*," and a magnificent yellow, green and orange thing called *Sunset at Ivry* by somebody named Guillaumin, which I never did find out how to pronounce.

My evening with the Impressionists did not really prepare me for Gauguin's stuff, though. There was one whole wall of dark nude native women, most of them lying down asleep. There was another just of self-portraits, which Luther later told me he had done by looking at himself in a mirror. Gauguin must have spent a lot of time looking at himself in the mirror. There were also huge paintings of blue trees and red pool halls, orange lakes and pink beaches, slightly grotesque animals and slightly strange people.

Luther and the boys were sitting off in the corner of one room of the museum, which was an old white stone building of many small rooms. They had grouped several folding chairs together in a circle. All but Preacher Hancock had a glass of red wine in his hand. All but Preacher Hancock and Luther were smoking cigarettes.

Luther, with little enthusiasm, motioned for me to grab a chair and join them. Jensen and Runyan, also with little enthusiasm, moved their chairs to make room for me.

"Gauguin died when he was fifty-four years old," Luther said. "We were just talking about being forty-four."

I said nothing.

"What should we call you?" Jensen the newspaperman said to me. He said it like it was a threat to my person.

"Mack. Everybody calls me Mack."

"How about Sir?" said Runyan. "I call everybody Sir."

"Whatever," I said.

"Reg here stayed in," Luther said. "The rest of us got out after three years. Reg stayed . . ."

"Until they kicked me out. They passed me over for lieutenant colonel and gave me the boot. You ever been passed over for anything, Mack?"

"No . . ."

"Being passed over is like being fired. Like being told everything you have worked for all your life finally added up to zip. I was told in a mimeographed letter from Headquarters Marine Corps in Washington. No real person even really signed it. It just came in the mail like a forty-five-rpm Record-of-the-Month circular. 'We regret to inform you, Runyan, Reginald Allen, Major, USMC, Serial Number 071279, that the promotion board declined to select you for lieutenant colonel.' "

"Don't expect any tears from politicians like Mack and me, Reg," Luther said. "The People are always passing us over for somebody else. You get used to it after a while."

"Or you run away," Runyan said.

"That's what Gauguin did," Jensen said. "He ran away from France to Tahiti. . . ."

"Because he had syphilis," said Luther. "Maybe he was running away to die."

Runyan said to me: "That's it. Go back to the States and tell everybody we came over here to die together of syph like real Marines should."

I said to Jensen: "Speaking of that, what did you do when that colonel told you to bring down the VD rate the way he did? You left me dangling. . . ."

"Well, the first thing I did was to say, 'Look, Colonel, we can relax a little bit about this because VD doesn't cripple much of anything besides the pecker, and when the war comes we're not going to try and screw the Red Chinese to death.' "

Everybody but me broke into guffaws of stupid laughing.

"I'm hungry," said Preacher Hancock. "Join us for dinner, Mack?"

. . .

Maybe he ran away to die, spoke the speaker of the House. So he was part of a suicide pact? He and four of his old Marine buddies had decided to kill themselves together? They came to France to do it? And to have one last fling?

No, no. No. I did not know about the others, but according to everything C. could find out, Luther did not have any reason to kill himself. He had no money, women, health or emotional problems. He was an Oklahoma man of family, position, reputation and substance.

The restaurant smelled of garlic, sausage and red wine. It was tiny and packed with people but they found room for the six of us back near the door to the kitchen. It was clear Luther and the boys had been there before. Maybe many times before. It was not for normal tourists. There were no tablecloths on the tables, the waitresses were older and casually dressed, there were no menus. What they served was written—in French, of course—in white chalk on a small blackboard.

The five talked to and among each other while we ate. And they told stories that it seemed to me all of them already knew because they had all been there when they happened. Runyan told one about stealing five buses from the Army on Okinawa to take the battalion to a beer party at a beach resort kind of place called Ishikawa. He said he and fifteen enlisted Marines went over to the Army motor pool at Fort Buckner and handed the people on duty there some phonied-up transportation requisition forms. When they took the buses back after the party, many had broken windows, some of the seats had been ripped up from the floor, and the buses reeked of beer and vomit. The other four men ate up the story like they had never heard it before. I didn't even see what was so funny about it. Why did Marines get such a charge out of stealing and fouling things that belonged to the Army? Weren't they both supposed to be on the same side?

I had always regretted not having served in the service, and it embarrassed me to have to say no when asked if I had been in the service. These guys were beginning to make me happy the armed forces of the United States did not take one-eyed people.

I ate something Jensen insisted I eat. It was called *cassoulet,* pronounced "cas-so-*lay*" (*let* is "lay" in French). It was a casserole-type thing of white beans cooked in a tomatoey juice with chunks of sausage, lamb and goose. Everyone but Preacher Hancock and I drank much red wine. Much, much red wine.

"We know why Preacher doesn't drink," Jensen said to me finally. "What's your problem, Mack?"

"It makes me drunk," I said.

Jensen broke up. He screamed and snorted and spit out his food and laughed and laughed so much he had to stop eating and drinking and wipe away the tears. That made Thornton giggle. Then Luther started. And so did Runyan. Preacher Hancock and I, the two sobers, were sitting across from each other at our round table. I saw the tickle of a smile begin to form around his mouth. It started happening to me, too. He laughed and then he giggled. So did I. He lost control. I lost control. Everybody lost control. We were six hooting, crying, crazy ninnies. And it went on and on and on. None of us could stop. My stomach began to hurt. Luther dumped sugar in what was left of my cassoulet. I stuck a piece of tomato from his salad into his right ear. Jensen fell over backward in his chair. Thornton poured some wine on Runyan's head. Runyan stuck a hunk of buttered Frenchy bread down the back of Thornton's shirt. On and on.

I had not acted like that since I grew up.

"This was what it was like every night in One-Nine," Jensen said to me after things had quieted down.

One-Nine?

"First Battalion, Ninth Marines, Mack. That was our outfit. We were the best. Right?"

"Right!" said the others almost in one voice.

Jensen grabbed me around the shoulders with his large left hand and arm. "Around this table sit the cream of the crop, Mack. We were it. I mean It. One-Nine was the Ready Battalion. The Ready Battalion. Ready to fight for America at the drop of a flag. Ready to hit the beaches, hit the Red Chinese, hit the Russians, hit whoever was in the American way. I was platoon leader of the Second Platoon, B Company. The finest, toughest, fastest thirty-eight men ever assembled in one leaky Quonset hut. I was their leader. I loved those kids. And they loved me. There

95

I was, just a kid out of college with new second lieutenant's bars. Suddenly I was responsible for the life and lives of thirty-eight other human beings. I was responsible for the way they dressed and ate and slept and marched and screwed. If they were sick, it was my problem. If they got a Dear John letter from home, it was my problem. Everything about them was my problem. I went from barely having responsibility for myself to being responsible for thirty-eight strangers. We all did. Every one of us around this table did. It helped me grow up like nothing else in this world could have. . . ."

"Let's go down to the water," Preacher Hancock said.

And before long we were walking barefoot in deep, wet white sand, carrying our shoes.

Runyan the career Marine fell in alongside me.

"I'll bet you would have made a good Marine, Mack," he said. "What were you?"

"Nothing." I pointed up to the black patch on my left eye. "Got to have two eyes to defend the United States of America."

"How did you lose it, Mack?"

I was tempted to lie. To say it was kicked out by Doak Walker in the 1947 TCU game or while I was tackling an escaped axe murderer or something. But I knew Luther knew better. So I told the truth. I told Runyan about watching the kick-the-can game in Kansas when I was sixteen and a half.

Runyan went crazy. "Kick-the-can! My God! It was

my favorite game! Hey, guys! Hey, Mack here lost his eye in a kick-the-can game!"

He insisted that we all play a game of kick-the-can. It took only a few minutes to find a can somebody had left in the sand. Runyan made himself It. We all went out and hid in the dark. He counted to ten.

We played until only Preacher Hancock and I were still standing. Luther and the others had one by one chosen to lie down on the sand and go to sleep.

· · ·

Before long the sun began to rise over the Mediterranean like an orange, red and blue Impressionist painting. Preacher Hancock and I sat on a rock down the beach from the others and watched it.

"Are you really a preacher?" I asked after a while.

"One hundred percent pure Methodist preacher," he replied. "A one-hundred-percent-pure unsuccessful Methodist preacher."

"Come on now," I said. "How can you be an unsuccessful Methodist? You people don't count converts and cleansed souls like we Holy Roads and the Baptists do."

Hancock, like Luther, looked like he had once been a Marine officer. He had no balloon around his middle, his skin was tight and tanned. He was at least six-two, maybe more. His hair was dark brown and thinning and gray but it didn't matter. He had presence. He reminded me a little bit of a CIA agent named Collins whom C. and I had had a spy adventure with once. If looks were all that mattered, they both could have been in television or in the movies.

"In the pulpit, I'm fine. Quietly inspirational, solid, accessible. I do all of the pastoral things extremely well. No parishioner gets a gallbladder out without a supportive visit from me. I can count and think, so the business side is no problem. Examine my skills and you would say, There goes a man of ministerial success. But it has not happened. I am like so many men of our times, Mack. I never realized the promise and the expectation. So here I am. That is the answer to your question, Why did you run away from home?"

"I didn't ask you that."

"Yes you did. It's like garlic on your breath. You reek of it."

"Does your wife know where you are?"

"I don't have a wife. That's my problem, Mack. You don't really mind if we call you Mack, do you?"

"No. Mack's fine. You're not a well ... you know ... a ..."

"A homosexual? No, no. I am just the opposite. I am a superheterosexual. You know what a nymphomaniac is? You must have nymphos in Oklahoma. Well, that's what I am. A male nympho. I have been married three times, and for a Methodist minister that is two too many. All three of those marriages came apart because I was intimate with women other than my wife. Lots of women other than my wife. I cannot help it, Mack. I have been to doctors and shrinks. I even took pills for a while. They were little blue plastic capsule things. I took them with the evening meal. They were supposed to suppress the sexual appetite. It didn't work. One guy at the Menninger Clinic..."

"That's in Topeka, Kansas. I was born in Kansas."

"Good for you. I live in Raleigh, North Carolina. Born and raised in Arizona, went to college in Colorado, came back from the Marines, went to seminary in Connecticut. I have worked in churches in South Carolina, Vermont, Florida, Minnesota, Iowa and California. The Menninger doctor said he would like to study me. He said he had never come across 'in the literature' such an example of *sexus extremiditus. Sexus extremiditus.* Ever been this close to one before in your life, Mack?"

"No, sir."

There was something about his story that had a smell of Tom Bell Pepper Bowen to it. Pepper, my friend and Jackie's first husband—the one who died in Korea—had been the best liar I had have ever come across. He could take a simple question like "How you doing, Pepper?" and turn it into an all-lies life story more interesting that Al Capone's, Stan Musial's and Harry Truman's combined.

"What happened at your get-together in Kansas City?" I asked Preacher Hancock.

He looked right at me for a one-two count and clearly decided not to answer my question. His eyes slid past me and beyond, to where the others were. "I see them moving over there," he said.

I glanced around. Luther was up on his feet, stretching his arms and legs.

"Up and at 'em, Marines!" Preacher Hancock yelled. Like a morning bugle call. "Time for breakfast!"

Breakfast.

. . .

I decided to skip breakfast altogether. In fact, I had about decided to skip the whole thing. Period. Sorry, Annabel, I failed. Your husband, the speaker of the House, ain't coming home. Not now, at least, maybe not ever. And for my money, Annabel, it may be just as well to leave him lost. He's gone green-eye crazy with several of his old Marine friends.

So I went back to the hotel when they went wandering, waddling, stretching off to another restaurant. How could they be that hungry, anyhow? It seemed to me like we had just eaten. Since I had gotten here it always seemed like we had just eaten.

There was a telephone message for me at the front desk. "Call C." was the message.

I went upstairs to my room and placed the call. The hotel operator, a female who seemed barely to understand English, said it would take a while. I lay down on my bed of red roses and fell immediately asleep.

About an hour later I was awake talking to C. in Oklahoma City.

"How's it going?" he asked. Again, he came through remarkably clear, if you consider how far France is from Oklahoma and it had to go over an ocean. We both had to talk precisely and loudly, but that was no problem.

"Lousy."

"Did you find them?"

"Yes, sir. They're certified loons. One of them's a Methodist preacher nympho."

There was static on the line.

"Where did she come from?" he yelled over it.

"It's a he!" I screamed back. "He said he took some blue pills for it."

"This is too expensive for jokes, Mack!"

"Serious!"

"The wife of the SSO man is on her way over to get him! I had to tell her we had found him, and where he was. That's why I called!"

"Tell her she's wasting her time!"

"Too late. She's gone. You okay?"

"I'm fine!"

"When you coming home?"

"In about five minutes maybe!"

The static went away. We could hear each other well again.

"Good," C. said. "The Chip's come up with another of his doozies to pull out the turnpike."

"What?"

"He's proposed naming them for two prominent live Oklahomans. Mickey Mantle, and Nita Pickens of Perkins Corner. He's now saying a vote against those two turnpikes is a vote against The Mick and Nita. The man's crazy."

I knew it was serious business, but I could not help but laugh. The graveyards of Oklahoma politics were full of people who had underestimated Joe Hayman of Buffalo. "You can call it crazy if you want to," I said. "Anything new on the Red River bus?"

"Not a thing. Nothing on the letter. Or anything else."

There was something about Luther and his strange Marine friends that had turned my thoughts about Buck Vermillion to something I could not put my finger on. Something about running away. Without really thinking about it, I said into the phone:

"Find out about the regulars. People who rode that schedule with Buck all of the time. Those who were on it when it crashed. Those who weren't. Okay?"

"Why?"

"I'm not sure."

"Okay. I'll do it. Did you really say Methodist preacher nympho a minute ago?"

"Yes. Good-bye for now."

6
. . .
ONWARD, CHRISTIAN SOLDIERS

Good-bye, France. Good-bye, Land of Bidets and Dirty Talk. Good-bye, Luther. Good-bye, Methodist Preacher Nympho and friends. I am going back to Oklahoma, where normal people come sweeping down the plains.

I tossed my few clothes and shaving gear into the soft, dark brown leather briefcase Jackie had given me for Christmas two years ago. It was slightly larger than a regular briefcase. I am sure she never dreamed that someday it would be used on a trip to France to retrieve Luther Wallace.

I paid my bill at the front desk with my American Express card—I had been a member since I became lieutenant governor—and went to find Luther to say "Good-bye, Luther."

There they came. All five of them. Marching down the narrow street toward the hotel in a single-file formation. A voice—it sounded like Jensen's—was calling out cadence. "Ah-one, tuh, threee, foe; ah-one, tuh, threee, foe; ah-one, tuh, threee, foe."

Their eyes were pointed straight ahead. Their shoulders were pulled back. Their stomachs were sucked in. Their heels hit the sandy asphalt together. They looked like old men acting like little boys playing soldier. And doing pretty well at it, I would have to admit. Even Thornton looked almost like a Marine could look. His balloon was still there but it didn't show as much.

"Squad, huh-alt!" Two hard thuds and they stopped. Right in front of me and the door to the hotel.

"Ley-yeft, face!"

They shuffled their feet. Now they were facing me at stiff attention. Their eyes, all five pairs, stared right by me.

It had been Jensen's voice, all right. He was the last one in the column. Now he barked: "Squad, dismissed!"

They relaxed and smiled and grabbed each other by hands and arms. They were so tickled with themselves.

Luther, his eye on my briefcase, held up a hand in a dramatically exaggerated command gesture to stop the noise. They all fell back into a loose attention. He addressed me in a booming voice like we were on a parade field or something: "Where are you headed, O Mr. Lieutenant Governor?"

"I am headed across the ocean for the Land Called

Oklahoma, O Mr. Speaker," I replied, also boomingly, playing along. "I take it you are not joining me?"

"You take it correctly, sir."

"Then good luck and, as they say, godspeed."

"We are going on a march, sir. You are, as they say, welcome to join us."

"No, thank you, sir. My duties are elsewhere."

"Oh, yes sir. Those duties entail charting exciting new routes for turnpikes to nowhere, in the Land Called Oklahoma, do they not, sir?"

"Precisely, sir. And addressing groups with names like Rotary, Lions and Kiwanis."

"It sounds like a kind of heaven, sir."

"It is, sir. It sure beats the dickens out of this."

"Where is the dickens, sir?"

"Between Oklahoma City and Tulsa on old Highway Sixty-six, sir."

"You must march to the dickens with us, sir."

"March, sir?"

"March, sir. We are marchers. In 1957 we had no war, but we had our march, sir."

"Your march, sir?"

"Around the island of Okinawa. One hundred twenty miles in five days, sir."

"You are going to march around Okinawa again, sir?"

"No, sir. Around here. Around France."

He was smiling. So were the others. So was I. It was crazy fun. The kind Luther and I often played back in Oklahoma.

What the dickens? Why not go on a little march with them before going back home?

What could be the harm in that?

• • •

We spent the next twenty minutes getting ready. For me that meant going around the corner to a kind of dime store and paying forty francs—about nine dollars—for some awful-looking black-and-white high-top tennis shoes and a pair of white sweatsocks, plus a couple of purple canvas belts to turn my briefcase into a backpack.

My enthusiasm went through some waning. "Exactly how long a march are we going on, anyhow?" I finally got around to asking Luther.

"As long as it takes," he said.

"Takes to do what?"

"To feel it."

It was an answer I should have thought about.

They put me in the middle of their single-file column. Luther was first, then Thornton, Jensen, me, Runyan and, bringing up the rear, Preacher Hancock.

"Move out!" Luther shouted.

I took my first steps right there behind Jensen. The pace was quick. Thornton started a singing chant that I vaguely remembered from somewhere—probably an old war movie.

> *"Go to ya left, ya right, ya left,*
> *Go to ya left, ya right, ya left.*
> *If I should die on a Russian shore, bay-eb,*

If I should die on a Russian shore, bay-eb,
If I should die on a Russian shore,
Bury me 'neath a Russian whore,
Honey, O bay-yay-be mine . . .
Go to ya left, ya right, ya left,
Go to ya left, ya right, ya left . . ."

The others joined in. Vigorously. Loudly. There were several verses. All smutty. I will not repeat them. Without really thinking about it, I joined in on choruses, which were fine.

We marched around the town square and out a street on one side. The French people paid us little mind. Six middle-aged American men marching single file through town singing a dirty American marching song was nothing special to pay attention to, I guess. A couple of kids waved to us. But even they didn't appear to think us really that strange.

I could not help but wonder about what kind of reaction there would have been in Adabel, Oklahoma, to six middle-aged Frenchmen marching single file through town singing a dirty French marching song.

After ten minutes or so, we were out of town heading north up a small hill with green trees and yellow flowers on the shoulder of a narrow two-lane blacktop road.

Jensen, whose broad back was constantly in sight of my one eye, started us singing "Alouette," which I knew from YMCA camp in Kansas. Then Luther got us on to "When Johnny Comes Marching Home Again." Each of us in turn was responsible for thinking of a song. I chose "Clementine," which from Runyan's groan behind me I could tell was probably not the Marines' idea of a marching song. But they all joined in.

"Break!" Luther yelled suddenly.

We moved over to a clump of sweet-smelling trees. We had been on the road almost an hour. Fifty minutes, to be exact. Runyan explained that we were following the standard Marine way to hike—keep a four-and-a-half-mile-an-hour pace with a ten-minute break every fifty minutes.

"How you doing there, Mack?" Luther said to me as I sat down.

"Great. Really great."

It was an honest answer. I felt some sweat under both arms. Something was beginning to rub against my left heel. But I felt great. I had never done anything like this before. I had never really hiked. Not in an organized-march way with other people. Not at the prescribed four-and-a-half-mile-an-hour pace with a ten-minute break every fifty minutes. Not the Marine way.

"I can't imagine what it must have been like to do this all day for five days around an island," I said to Thornton, who had sat down next to me. He was sweating profusely. His face was red.

"Finishing that was the best thing I ever did," he said. "Only half of the battalion finished. Including the officers. It's in our official records. It's in *us*."

"I didn't really finish it," Jensen said. "But it wasn't

my fault. I had blisters so bad my socks were soaked in blood."

"Remember Coppelli from Bravo Company? He finished walking in his shower shoes," Thornton said.

"Up yours, fat boy," Jensen said.

"Fat calling the kettle fat, I'd say, Mr. Tub of Lard."

"I still want to know what you did about that VD problem," I said quickly to Jensen.

He was happy to change subjects. And to tell a story. He said: "Well, I decided to try the tried-and-true Marine way. Humiliation. Public humiliation. I had a big blackboard erected in front of our battalion headquarters hut. Every time a new case of VD turned up, we would call a battalion formation in front of it. Everybody lined up, like for an inspection by companies and platoons. Then the individual Marine who'd gotten the new case of clap was called—by name—to come front and center in front of his whole world. Private U. S. Jones, front and center! He'd march smartly out of his place at rigid attention to the blackboard. Then he'd write his name and the VD case in the battalion he was, the number he was. If there were already forty-five cases, say, he'd write in huge letters 'Jones' and then the number forty-six. I could not think of anything worse. There, in complete silence in front of his buddies and all officers of the battalion, he had to humiliate himself. I could not imagine a better deterrent to clap."

"That must have stopped it in its tracks, all right," I said.

"It was a disaster. It didn't stop a thing. In fact, it made things worse. The troops started cheering after every new Blackboard March. That's what they started calling it— Blackboard March. Attaway, Marine! Rah, rah, rah! Give 'em hell, One-Nine! Let's be number one! Get out there and catch VD! Rah, rah, rah! Semper Fi! It was a god-damn disaster. . . ."

"Saddle up!" Preacher Hancock yelled. He and Luther had switched places.

We stood up and moved back to the shoulder of the road.

"All right, let's move out!" Hancock shouted.

And all right, we moved out.

. . .

I noticed after another thirty minutes or so that Jonas Jensen was favoring his right leg. A tiny limp developed in his stride.

"You okay?" I yelled up to him.

"Just these shoes," he said. He was wearing a pair of low-cut white tennis shoes. "Hiking is as much about shoes as it is anything. How about you?"

"I'm fine." Which was almost a lie. I could feel a blister growing down there on my left heel. But it wasn't enough yet to worry about. Or mention.

The terrain was now flat and the shoulder of the road was wide enough for us to walk two abreast. In a few minutes Jensen fell back alongside me on my right. His face had reddened. He was puffing a bit.

"You think we're crazy, don't you?" he said.

"If you're crazy, I'm crazier," I said with feeling. "I'm right here with you."

"I wondered if marching like this would bring it back."

"What back?"

"One-Nine. Being something that mattered."

"Don't newspapermen matter?"

"Not me."

We were in the center of a village when breaktime came a short while later. It was a gorgeous little place. The narrow streets were paved in old stone and they curved up and around tiny churches and squares and gardens that looked like they had been there since life began. The houses and shops were right up against the street and their fronts were mostly painted blue and pink and yellow. In the shop windows were strings of sausages and dressed chickens, magnificent meringue and chocolate desserts, scrumptious cheeses and breads. The Impressionist painters could definitely have lived there. So could Santa Claus and most anybody else who wanted just to be happy.

Preacher Hancock led us to a spot under some trees right on the town square. As in La Napoule, the people of the village paid us little or no mind. What was so unusual about five crazy former U.S. Marines and one crazy current one-eyed lieutenant governor of Oklahoma taking a ten-minute hike break on the town square?

I felt the need to examine my left heel. I pulled off the shoe and the white sock. There was a blister there, all right. It was about the size of a nickel. Very red on the bottom but with the skin on top very white and loose, about to break. Pus and blood were only minutes away from my sock.

"You need one of these." It was Luther. He was standing over me with a Band-Aid in his hand. I took it and put it on my blister.

"We're all going to have them," Luther said. "It's the name of this game."

Yes sir, Mr. Marine.

I got Jensen to continue his VD story. I was like I was when I was a kid, when I'd go to Coffeyville, Kansas, to see my grandmother on my mother's side. She'd start a Bobbsey Twins story the first night before bed and then read the rest of it piece by piece until the story was over and I had to go back home to Medicine Bend. It made me look forward to going to bed, which, of course, was the whole point of the exercise. Now Jensen and his struggles as VD Control officer of One-Nine were having the same effect on me.

Turn the page, Jensen.

"Well, the colonel went absolutely ape-nuts over the Blackboard March result. He would have had me court-martialed and demoted and deballed if he could have. I pleaded for one more chance. I decided I had to play rough. I had the Navy corpsmen assigned to the battalion requisition or steal several cases of penicillin tablets. Penicillin will knock out clap. It's about the only thing that will. If it's taken right away it works real wonders. We had it available for everyone, but taking it was voluntary.

And nobody did. So I had all Officers of the Day and NCOs of the Day armed with forty-fives loaded with live ammunition. And every Marine, no matter what rank, religion or national origin, was forced from then on to take two penicillin tablets whenever he returned from liberty. He had to take them with a sip of water from a paper cup right there in front of the OOD or NCOD. No exceptions. We had a couple of goody-good Baptists in the battalion raise some hell, and then the Protestant and Catholic chaplains complained to the colonel about forcing young Marines to take two penicillin tablets after returning from chapel. I agreed to stop it, but then I just ignored it. You can get clap on the way home from church just like on the way from anywhere else. But it didn't work, either. The troops beat my system again."

"How? With armed men staring at them and all of that?" I said with genuine interest. Will the Bobbsey Twins be all right, Grandmother?

"The troops found a way to hold the tablets in their mouth and only swallow the water. They'd leave the hut and spit them out. Somebody had spread the word—the correct word—that a lot of penicillin also tended to switch off the sex drive. So nobody wanted to take that chance. Never ever underestimate the ability of an otherwise idiot young U.S. Marine to defeat any system. It comes natural to them. . . ."

"Hey, Luther, how about spending some real time here in this place?" Runyan yelled. "This is right off a post-card. . . ."

"Forget it. We're on a march." It was Thornton. Idiot!

And it was Thornton who shouted, "Saddle up!"

And then, "Move out!"

So we were changing leaders every break? So he was anxious to serve his turn? So it had been a long time since he had led anybody doing anything except at the SSO in Pawnee City, Oklahoma?

In the new formation Luther and I found ourselves walking side by side.

"Jensen is hurting," I said after a while.

"We all will be before long," he said.

"Then what?"

He looked over at me and smiled. And shrugged. And moved up and away to a single-file position in front of me.

"It's coming," said Runyan. He said it quietly. He was right behind me. I slowed my pace until he was beside me on the right.

"What's coming?" I asked. Runyan's face looked like a Halloween mask of an ugly old lady witch in agonizing pain. The color was a cross between fresh concrete and a freshly soiled baby's diaper.

"Wine," he said. "Breakfast. My guts. Everything."

And he threw up. Fortunately, to his right, away from me. While he moved. Without slowing his pace.

"Hey, let's stop a second," I said, trying to keep from gagging and throwing up myself. Other people's throwing up always made me gag. Always.

Runyan motioned me away. He kept throwing up and he kept walking.

I had a weak stomach. It had always been hard for me to be around somebody throwing up—even Jackie or one of the kids—and not do it myself. I felt it coming. I looked away.

Preacher Hancock was behind us. I looked around for help. For something. He just smiled and kept walking.

Clearly, throwing up was not enough to stop a U.S. Marine.

It was all so crazy.

At that moment an Arkansas River of nausea rushed into my stomach and throat. I had no breakfast, no lunch, no nothing to throw up and out. I dry-heaved. And coughed up yellow spit. I did it again. And again. And again. Until there was nothing left to even spit. Nothing but my insides.

And I kept walking.

When I had stopped heaving and spitting and I was still walking, I felt a hand on my left shoulder. It was Luther. My friend, the Runaway Speaker of the Oklahoma House of Representatives. He had come back to watch me throw up, obviously.

"Nice going, Mack," he said.

Nice going, Mack.

Crazy, crazy, crazy, Mack.

. . .

Lunch break. Chowtime, being what my friends from One-Nine called it. We stopped in front of a small café that was also a grocery store and a bar and a service station. It wasn't really a town, only a crossroads, or what in Oklahoma and Kansas we would call a corner. Like Elmdale Corner, Bill's Corner, Gridley Corner or Perkins Corner, home of Nita Pickens, Miss Country Music.

Nobody inside the store spoke English, so Preacher Hancock, who knew at least how to eat in French, went in and bought six ham and cheese sandwiches on small loaves of French bread. Jensen spoke French much better but he went directly to some grass and lay down. His face was getting redder and redder. So were his eyes.

Runyan's and my problems had destroyed my appetite. All I could do was think of me marching along that road at full speed while tossing my insides for all to see. It eliminated even the possibility of eating a ham and cheese sandwich on French bread. Maybe forever.

I found another piece of grass and sat down. My left heel had really begun to hurt. The Band-Aid had stopped doing the job. I pulled it off and with it came a hunk of skin. The blister underneath was now the size of a quarter. It was raw and bloody red.

Thornton the SSO man was in even worse shape. He took off both of his shoes and socks. He had broken bloody blisters on his toes, too. I was amazed he could still walk.

"They've been worse than this many times," he said. But he said it slowly. Like reciting a piece to class in the fourth grade.

Luther came around and checked us both out. So did Preacher Hancock. They had Band-Aids and words. I knew neither was going to help.

"You take a pill for blisters, too?" I asked Preacher. Trying to be funny.

"I work out every day. Run, play tennis or handball. Have for years."

I didn't have to ask Luther anything. I already knew that he was a physical fitness nut, too. Every day there he'd been, in sweats and sneakers running around the capitol. It was as much a part of the scenery as the pumping oil wells on the capitol grounds that got so much attention from out-of-state tourists. The in-state tourists got just as much of a kick out of watching their speaker jog. My view of jogging had always been that most people did it to show off. There were a lot of other less boring ways to get rid of fat and develop shin splints than running in public. It was the need to exhibit hairy legs and other half-clothed and moving bodily parts that motivated a lot of people. Maybe not Luther. *Certainly* not Luther. But many of the others.

"You want to know something?" Thornton whispered after Luther and Preacher left. "This is the first serious exercise like this I have done since I got out of the Corps twenty-two years ago. The day I got out was the day I swore I would never do anything like this again. And here I am."

I had nothing to say to him about that.

Following the rules for a chow break, we were back on our feet and moving out thirty minutes later.

Runyan was now leading the column. Jensen, looking worse than when we stopped, followed him. Then came Thornton, Preacher, me and Luther.

The pace was now just over half as fast as it was when

we had left La Napoule. Runyan kept adjusting for Jensen, who seemed to get slower and slower with every step. I noticed also that Runyan himself was limping slightly. Thornton, favoring both of his blistered feet, had started to shuffle.

"How about another song?" Luther yelled up from the rear.

"Start it yourself!" Runyan shouted back.

"I've got one," Preacher said. And he sang:

> *"Onward, Christian soldiers,*
> *Marching as to war,*
> *With the Cross of Jesus,*
> *Going on before.*
> *Christ, the royal Master,*
> *Leads against the foe;*
> *Forward into battle,*
> *See His banners go. . . ."*

Luther joined in. So did I and the other Christian soldiers.

Five or six minutes later, way early for a regular break, we abruptly stopped. Like we had run into a wall that would not give.

Thornton, our leader, was sitting down on the dirt roadside. I moved up to him. So did the others.

He took off his left shoe and sock. There was a mass of blood covering his heel. He took off his right shoe and sock. There was an even larger and bloodier mess.

Calmly, silently, with precision, he removed a pocket-knife from his knapsack and cut away a hole in the back of each shoe and sock. Then he put them back on and stood up.

"Forget it, Bobby," Runyan said to him. "We'll go get a car and come back for you."

"Saddle up!" Thornton screamed. Like a lunatic.

He took off in a painful limp. And we followed him in single file.

Within ten minutes we were barely moving. Our rate of march could not have been more than a mile and a half an hour.

"When do you make him stop?" I asked Luther. "When his feet are gone and he's down to nothing but bloody stumps for legs?"

"It's all up here," Luther said, tapping a finger to his head.

"Those blisters and that blood are down there, Luther." I pointed to my feet.

Preacher drifted back to Luther and me.

"Maybe we should call it quits for the day, Luther?" he said. "Bobby's about through. Jonas is worse. Runyan's not much better. How about you, Mack?"

My left foot was hurting badly. Something was developing on my right, too.

"I'm just great," I said.

Luther moved up and talked to Runyan and then to Jonas and finally to Thornton.

We stopped for the night. Even though it was not yet three in the afternoon.

Luther and Preacher were our leaders now. They were

our commanders, the first two among what had been equals when we started. I wondered if it was only because they and their feet were in good physical shape. Would it have been that way if they, like Thornton, were shuffling around with their bloody heels showing through holes in the back of their shoes? Or if like Jonas Jensen and, increasingly now, Runyan, their faces were in an awful flush and puff of agony and pain?

Thornton, with Preacher's assistance, had guided us off the narrow road into a grove of apple trees. There we camped. Or in Runyan's words, crapped out. Each of us had taken a blanket from the La Liberté. We spread them out on the ground in a loose circle.

I helped Jensen lay his out. He dropped down on it like he might never get up.

Thornton looked very sick. There was deep red in his eyeballs, and his lips were almost a light shade of blue. But there he was, trying to maintain his bearing, the appearance of a man still together and able. The man from Pawnee City, Oklahoma, was not going to quit.

Runyan, who had stayed in the Marine Corps twenty-four years, seemed ready to quit. There was something coming into his fat flushed face besides pain. He wanted to know how he and the rest of us came to be doing such an absolutely insane thing. Maybe I wanted to see it and just imagined it. Anybody looking closely at me would have had no trouble reading that message in my one-eyed face. Loud and clear. I knew at that moment of only one person in the whole world who was nuttier than these five men on this road in France. Me.

Luther and Preacher went off in search of a farmhouse or a farmer or a somebody, to make sure it was all right to make ourselves at home in the apple orchard. They left the rest of us lying on our blankets like wounded on the road to Gettysburg or Guadalcanal.

"What is the point of this?" I said from my position on my back, lying on my blanket. I said it loudly enough for all to hear. I said it straight up to the sky to everyone.

"Suicide," Bob Thornton said, also to the sky. "Jonas said we came out here to kill ourselves."

I said: "I thought Marines killed other people, not themselves. Jonas, why are you here, really?"

Silence.

"Jonas! Hey, Jonas. Why did you run away to France?" I yelled.

Still no answer. I sat up and looked over to see if he was still breathing. He was.

"Runyan? How about you?" I called out.

"It's none of your business," he replied.

"Yes, it is. My blisters are just as bloody and terrible as yours."

"Look, Mr. Lieutenant Governor," Thornton said. "You are . . ."

"Mack, for God's sake. Mack! My name is Mack!"

"All right, Mack. You are the lieutenant governor of Oklahoma. I used to be First Lieutenant Robert Thornton, USMC, 071276, Commander, First Platoon, Bravo Company, First Battalion, Ninth Marines. Now all I am is a manger of an SSO in Pawnee City."

"The *Star*'s forcing me out." It was Jonas, almost in a

whisper. "They say they need new blood on the national desk. They're giving me three months to find a job or move into Action Line. You know about Action Line? People who can't get their trash picked up call Action Line. I am a newspaperman and I will not help people get their trash picked up."

Nobody said anything for a few minutes. It was Runyan's turn, of course. "Runyan? What about you?" I yelled finally. "Why are you here?"

"The stories. I came to hear the stories. Jonas's stories. Jonas, tell him the one about Christmas Eve."

Jonas said, "You want to hear about Christmas Eve, Mack?" I didn't but I said nothing. So he said:

"Arkie Adams started it all. There must have been twenty or thirty of us from One-Nine. It was Christmas Eve and it was raining and we were all alone with nothing else to do, so we put on coats and ties and went over to the Officers' Club at the Air Force base there on Okinawa for a Christmas Eve dance. The Air Force could have dependents with them. You know, wives and kids and things. So there we were for a while, sitting at tables around the dance floor watching the Air Force guys dance. Behaving ourselves mostly, drinking and singing carols. Things like that. But after a while Arkie went out there on the dance floor and tried to cut in on some Air Force guy. Then somebody else went out and did it. Then some more. Finally there must have been ten of us out there on the dance floor all tapping Air Force guys on their shoulders. This Filipino singer who sounded exactly like

June Christie kept singing June Christie songs like "Moon over Miami" and Christmas songs like "White Christmas" and the fifty-four-piece band kept playing and there we were. The Air Force guys wouldn't stand aside, of course, because they weren't dancing with strangers or pick-ups. Those women were their wives or fiancées or daughters and things like that.

"Arkie left the dance floor and made a move on the Christmas tree. Remember that sucker, Reg? It was at least twelve feet tall. It was full of pastel green and blue and lights and shiny crinkly round ornaments. Arkie took an ornament off and crushed it in his hand like it was cellophane paper. Somebody else came over and grabbed an ornament and threw it on the dance floor like it was a hand grenade. Before long all of us were around the tree with Arkie. Some of the guys threw ornaments down on the floor and cracked them like pecans with their boots. We had all worn our boots because it was raining. The Air Force guys began to get upset and frisky. Enough of them were drunk and enough of us were drunk that before long there was some pushing and shoving and tripping over broken Christmas tree ornaments. A few punches were thrown. And it wasn't too long after that that a group of Army and Air Force officers in uniforms with MP armbands came in blowing whistles and acting tough.

"There was a big investigation afterward. They were trying to pin action-unbecoming-an-officer-and-a-gentleman charges against Arkie. We all had to give statements. I remember swearing that I could not remember if Arkie was even there. That's what most of us did. They finally put something in Arkie's service jacket about it, but that was all. Merry Christmas. That was the worst Merry Christmas of my life."

"What happened to Arkie afterward?" I asked. "After the Marines? Or did he stay in . . ."

"Well, I heard he went to law school at the University of Virginia or some place like that and went into the FBI," Runyan said.

Jensen said: "I tried to find him for the reunion and never did. Maybe he went undercover somewhere looking for bank robbers and never came out."

I said, "So this was what you all talked about in Kansas City?"

"War. We also talked a lot about war," Thornton said. "About combat. About dodging snipers and zigzagging through mortar and heavy machine-gun fire. About calling in close air support and artillery rounds close to our own troops. About following orders, even though it meant certain death. About digging foxholes in frozen ground with machine-gun fire all around. About going hand to hand with Chinks, Koreans and other Slant-Eyes. About medals and courage and bravery. About never giving up. About sticking in there with blood and mud in your eyes and nose. About dying. About bringing out our casualties. Our dead and wounded. About being real Marines. . . ."

It brought me to a sitting position. "Wait a minute," I said. "You guys weren't in combat."

"That's right. But we would have been great if we had

of been. Right, Reg? Reg was in the real thing in Vietnam."

Runyan said: "One-Nine would have been terrific in combat. No question. Amen."

"Amen," Thornton said.

"Amen," Jensen said.

I lay back down.

7

. . .

SEMPER FI

LUTHER and Preacher came back with the proper permissions. They also had six loaves of bread the French call *baguettes,* several hunks of weird-smelling cheeses and three bottles of red wine with no labels on the bottles. Eventually each of us took some of everything and ate.

After that Thornton started singing again, with everyone but Preacher and me joining in.

The songs were absolute filth. Grossly, sickeningly so. They were mostly about various parts of women and various kinds of sexual acts. They were nothing but pornographic, obscene awfulness set to music. I was stunned, frankly, to know that songs like them even existed. I wondered who wrote them—and why. I wondered whether they were ever published as sheet music or put out on little 45 records. I wondered why the OBI and the

FBI and the other I's of this world didn't stop it, if they were.

It was the first thing I asked Luther about later, when we got away for a walk and a talk. How in the world could grown, so-called civilized adult men sing songs like that? He said filthy talk was a way of life and communication among Marines. He said the words have lost their real meaning so they're not really dirty anymore. I told him filth was always filth. Even after you got used to it.

I remembered what Pepper had said about the Marines. In one of his letters to me from boot camp before he went to Korea to die, he said the best he could tell, the Marines were training him to cuss the Red Chinese to death.

It was not really dirty Marine songs I wanted to talk to Luther about when I suggested late in the evening that maybe we could take a little walk together, just the two of us. I said my feet were up to it if his were.

"I've got it now for everybody but you," I said finally, introducing the real subject.

"Got what?"

We were walking down a dirt road Luther said went to a barn belonging to the farmer who owned the place. Luther said he was a nice man for a Frenchman.

"Why they ran away from home without telling anybody."

"I told you. Don't look for any mysteries, Mack. That is all there is. It's like filling up a pail with water. Once it's filled, it takes no more and it spills over. I was filled to the top and it spilled over. Way over."

"Are you ever going home?"

"Probably."

"When?"

"I have no idea."

There was one particular part of what he was saying that really did not add up, "You say you were sick of being responsible. Okay, fine. But look at you now. What's so unresponsible about this? You and that preacher are running things with great responsibility like we were in some kind of life-and-death struggle."

"Don't try to understand this, Mack. I don't myself."

"Is it singing filthy songs? You big grown men ran away from home so you could yodel away vile things about women and the sex act while marching along together through France? Oh me, oh my, how big and unresponsible you are. If that's all this is about, why didn't you just close your door at the capitol and sing away to your heart's content?"

"That's not what this is about."

"What is it, then?"

"Jonas said, Let's run away. He said he knew a place in France. I thought, Why not? And here we are. It's not that complicated."

"You are the speaker of the House of Representatives, Luther. That is a position of power and prestige. It's important work you do. . . ."

"Oh, yes, sir. What could be more important in the world than killing unneeded turnpikes in Oklahoma? I just wanted to run away and be a Marine again. So I did.

That's all there is to it. I haven't done anything like this since I was five years old and I emptied the water out of the goldfish aquarium in kindergarten and killed two goldfish. Nothing. I have always done the right and responsible thing. Always. Good student, good son, good nephew, good grandson, good athlete, good student-body president, good boyfriend, good husband, good father, good grandfather, good citizen, good politician, good legislator, good speaker, good man, good person, good turnpike-killer, good, good, good."

"Again, what about Annabel and your kids and the citizens of Oklahoma? They're good people, too, you know."

"F—— you, Mack."

He said it calmly, quietly, like he was asking me to pass the salt and pepper. We had come to the barn, but there was no point in going in. We had nothing else to talk about.

We turned around and headed back down the dark silent road to our campsite.

· · ·

I had slept on the ground only three times in my life: when I was eleven at the YMCA camp outside Chanute, Kansas, and twice on Cub Scout campouts with my son Tommy Walt, now the twenty-seven-year-old entrepreneur owner of T.W. Grease Collectors, Inc., Oklahoma's largest restaurant-grease collection business. In three years he had built it from a one-employee, one-pickup operation in Oklahoma City to a thirty-seven-employee, sixteen-

vehicle statewide enterprise with branch offices in Tulsa,
Enid, Lawton and Muskogee. He even had been thinking
lately about expanding down into the North Texas border
towns of Sherman, Denison, Gainesville and Wichita
Falls. The business was collecting old, used-up restaurant
grease in big metal drums and selling it to rendering plants
for making soap and similar things. I must confess I did
not even know there was such a business until Tommy
Walt went into it.

Here now, for the fourth time when I laid me down
on the ground, it was on ground covered with thick green
grass off the side of a narrow blacktop road somewhere
in southern France. I had not enjoyed anything at all about
the first three times. The Y camp sleep-out had been awful
because it had rained all night and the counselors, most
of whom were students at teachers colleges learning how
to be junior high football coaches, thought sleeping in the
rain would help build our characters. The two campouts
with Tommy Walt had been really terrible. The first one
because Tommy Walt had been so scared he would be
bitten by a copperhead snake he'd wet his pants and
sleeping bag. He'd then made me tell the other scouts
and fathers that the wetness was caused by a cup of coffee I had spilled. I am sure the odor gave it away. The
second campout, the next year, had been even worse. One
of the fathers was a Republican orthopedic surgeon and
shopping-mall investor who hated me, Governor Hayman
and all Democrats, governments, blacks, Catholics, teachers, foreigners, weathermen, columnists, truckers, diplo-

mats, movies, books, television shows, unions, osteopaths, dentists, chiropractors and architects. I never took the politics part of politics very seriously except when some idiot forced me to. This guy did. I told him he was a fascist Nazi brownshirt right-wing fanatic un-American swine who did not understand the first thing about freedom, liberty, democracy, Jesus, the United States of America or the State of Oklahoma. Unfortunately for Tommy Walt, I told the idiot this at the top of my lungs while we were all sitting around a campfire. And I threw a cellophane bag of marshmallows at him when I did. The marshmallows flew out of the bag and went all over the surgeon and the ground. Tommy Walt again wet his pants and sleeping bag and later he quietly resigned from the Cub Scouts. Which at least meant no more campouts and sleeping on the ground.

Until now, until France.

The tan Hôtel La Liberté blanket was thin but it did not matter. The grass underneath was like a soft, comfortable bed of cotton that smelled like a flowery brand of aftershave instead of like grass, as grass did in Oklahoma. Maybe the French mixed perfume in with their manure?

I went to sleep admiring a bright round moon and a sky of tiny stars. It was both comforting and unsettling to think that Jackie and the kids and the rest of the people of Oklahoma, six thousand miles away, could look up and see the same moon and stars. But what about the seven-hour time difference? It was still daylight in Oklahoma, so how could they look up and see the same moon and stars?

It was a reminder of how much I did not know. And probably never would know.

Back in Oklahoma, Luther had always been a constant reminder of that. He knew so much more about everything than I did. Things that mattered, at least. Like music. I knew some of the country people, like Nita Pickens, and I listened to the pop singers, but I had never sat through an entire symphony concert. We had a symphony there in Oklahoma City, and I do not think they ever played once when Luther was not right there in the front row acting like they were playing only for him in a language only he understood. I went with him twice but both times I fell asleep in a few minutes. It made me feel like an ignorant hick, but there was nothing I could do about it. Violins playing music I did not know or appreciate did that to me. Worse, though, was what I did not know about history and philosophy things. One time Luther and I were in a meeting with Buffalo Joe and some others, talking about going on a weekend retreat somewhere to have a frank and open discussion about the future of Oklahoma. Luther said we might want to bring somebody in who was experienced in the Socratic method. He said they used it at his law school in Massachusetts and it worked beautifully at getting people to open up. I said, What's the Socratic method all about? He said, You know, Mack, Socratic like in Socrates. Who? I said. Socrates, he said. He must have been before my time, because I never heard of him or his method, I said. Everybody laughed at me. Everybody but Luther. After the meeting he said he would bring me a book to read about Socrates, because everybody should know about him. He brought me the book and I tried to read it, but I simply did not know enough to follow what he was all about. The worst thing about it was knowing that I never would know about classical music or Socrates. Or Impressionist art or so many other things like that. It made me sometimes think the whole education system should be switched around. Stop school in about the eleventh grade and force people to go to work for a while. Then, after four or five years, when they knew what they wanted or needed to know, they would pick up with school again. I remember after the Korean War hearing about the vets who came back and went to college on the GI Bill. Guys who were lousy students in high school became great college students because they knew what they needed to know and appreciated the opportunity to learn it.

I talked to Luther about all of this one night after a late session of the legislature, while we were waiting for the House Appropriations Committee to make up its mind about a road-and-bridge budget. He said he considered me an extremely intelligent man. Some of the dumbest people he knew, he said, were jerks who had not entertained a new idea or had a fresh thought since the day they walked off the stage with their big-time diploma in their hot little hand that pronounced them well-educated. They could hum along with Beethoven and quote Socrates, but they had no sense of right or wrong or of people or worth or humanity like I did.

I think he said it to make me feel better. Which it did.

· · ·

I woke up to a feeling of peace and well-being. That lovely smell was still in the grass. Now the early-morning sun had brought a dark orange to go with it. And somebody had either made or gone off and bought some coffee. Or the marvelous smell of it, at least. I took a while to focus on where I was and what I was doing. *Where* was France, a place where World War II was fought and french fries were invented. *What* was marching with five old men who were trying to go back to being young Marine lieutenants again in something they called One-Nine. One of the five was an honest and intelligent friend of mine from Oklahoma, a fellow high official of the government of the Sooner State.

I had to go relieve myself. I sat up and then moved to stand up on my left foot and leg. The pain was so sharp I almost yelled out. It felt like somebody had cut a hole in my foot with a rotary drill bit. And I was still barefoot. I could not imagine how I ever again would be able to put a shoe on that foot. It was bad enough having no left eye. Now I was also not going to have a left foot.

But I had to go. So I limped and shuffled off away from the others. I nodded and grunted at Luther and Preacher, both of whom were up and about, of course. Thornton, Runyan and poor Jensen were still lumps under their tan Hôtel La Liberté blankets.

135

When I returned from the woods, Runyan and Thornton were also sitting up. And soon they were all talking about the 120-mile hike around Okinawa. All except Jonas, who was still down and asleep. Or out.

"I think the colonel wanted the battalion to get some kind of special citation," Thornton said.

"I thought we did get something," Luther said.

"Just in our individual service jackets," Preacher said. "I saw it in mine. Big as life. 'Completed hundred-twenty-mile hike, First Battalion, Ninth Marines, 7 September 1957.' I felt for the guys who didn't finish. Particularly the officers."

"I would have if I had not been ordered back into camp to deal with a legal case," Runyan said. "I was the legal officer, remember."

"I remember," Preacher said. "I didn't mean you. I mean guys who fell out. Like Jonas. Or Nelson over in Weapons Company. I have never seen a set of blisters on two feet like he had. They were on the bottom of his feet as well as the heels and toes. All bleeding and full of pus."

"I came within ten minutes of not finishing," Thornton said, looking down at his own blisters. "It was like I am now, only worse. If I had had to go another hundred yards it would have been over. I would have collapsed right there in front of my troops and the colonel and God."

"But you didn't," Luther said. "That is the point."

"I have never felt as good as I did when we walked back into the battalion area that afternoon," Thornton said. "I've been waiting for thirty years for something else that great to happen to me."

"It's not the same as combat," Runyan said, "but it's right up there close."

"Hear, hear," Luther said.

"Semper Fi!" It was Jonas Jensen. Sitting up, full voiced.

"Hey, Jonas! Semper Fi!" Thornton screamed. And the others joined in. "Semper Fi! Semper Fi! Semper Fi!"

"Semper Fi," I knew from Pepper's time, was what Marines said to each other. It comes from *semper fidelis,* which means "always faithful" in Latin.

We were all drinking coffee heavy with cream and sugar out of little white Styrofoam cups. Runyan hurriedly poured another and took it over to Jensen, who was smiling and blinking and laughing like a normal person again.

The five of them then reached and stepped forward and around to click their cups together like they were glasses of champagne or steins of Bud.

"When are you going to finish the VD Control story?" I said to Jensen.

"Now," he said. "Right now. I had a stroke of hardball genius. I mean *hard* hardball. I announced at a battalion formation that effective that date I, as VD Control Officer, would write a personal letter home to the wife or mother of each Marine who got VD. I would inform that wife or mother that I regretted to inform her that her husband or son had contracted a dreaded disease called gonorrhea, or crabs, or whatever. I was pleased to inform her, however, that her husband or son was undergoing excellent medical treatment, the best the U.S. Marine Corps and the Department of the Navy could provide, and there was no danger to the Marine she undoubtedly loved so very much. In other words, the Marines have landed, the situation is under control. Semper Fi and all of that. But then I said I would say in the letter that she should also know that some strains of some venereal diseases do tend to recur months or even years afterward. As a VD Control officer I would advise her to initiate a vigorous appropriate preventative health program once her Loved-One Marine returned to her. I told the battalion that I intended to close each letter by saying all of this was confidential and she should not mention this to her Loved-One Marine in the mail. That might cause a morale problem."

He paused for me to ask, What happened? But I didn't have to.

"Our VD rate fell to less than five percent. And I think that five percent really did come from toilet seats. Those young Marines were trained for the priesthood by the time they went home."

There were laughs all around. From me, too.

"Tell him the final kicker," Runyan said.

"Now that is really none of his business," Jensen said. "I wish I'd never told you. Or anyone else."

I waited and waited for Jensen or one of the others to tell the story, but he didn't.

And before long we had saddled up and moved out. The order of march was Luther, Thornton, Jensen, me, Runyan, and Preacher. There had been no conversation before we left about where we were going or how long we were going to march. I hadn't brought it up. There was nobody to ask, because nobody knew. Not even Luther. I had a feeling it could end in twenty minutes or it could go on forever.

Luther, constantly looking back, mostly at Jensen, had started us moving ever so slowly. Jensen walked right next to me. He shuffled his huge body forward like there were lead weights on each foot. But he was talking again, as if the words were giving him the energy to move his feet and legs.

"You found us through my ex-wife, huh?" he said.

"That's right," I said.

"I was a Marine when we met. She was a schoolteacher down at Parris Island in South Carolina. I came back there from One-Nine and Okinawa for six months before I got out. She thought I was something special. A Marine in dress blues. Going to be a newspaperman. Travel the world. All we ever did was live in Overland Park."

"Overland Park."

"Kansas City suburb. She hated what I didn't become. So did I. She could divorce me. I couldn't."

His face lost some of its color. He was sweating heavily.

"Do you want to sit down a minute?" I said.

"I'm fine," he said. "We hadn't gotten off to a really great start, to be honest about it. Which is the rest of the VD story I probably shouldn't tell you. But I'm thinking you're almost one of us now, Mack. Do the people in Oklahoma, the regular people, really call you Mack?"

"When they call me anything. Being the lieutenant governor is not something that gets you mobbed on the streets of Tulsa. Are you sure you don't want to take a break?"

Jensen motioned with his head toward Thornton, who was right in front of us. "He's the one to watch. I've seen a few people looking like he looks. It usually means bad things could happen."

"Why won't he stop, then?" Jensen shrugged his shoulders.

"You want to stop talking?" I asked. "Conserve energy . . ."

"No, no. I'm fine. I'm fine. I caught a dose of clap myself. That's the end to my VD Control officer story. The unwritten gentleman's agreement is that officers didn't catch VD. We were not counted in the numbers or reported to any headquarters. Nobody talked about it. We went to the corpsmen and the Navy doctors in off-duty hours. So I was able to keep it a secret. Particularly from the colonel, the battalion commander. I don't even want to think of what he would have hung me from, and by what, if he had known. He never found out. And everything was fine. I ate penicillin tablets like they were Life Savers, and it went away. I went back to the States, to Parris Island, and like I said, met my wife-to-be. Then two weeks before the wedding I suffered a Return of the Clap. It was a terrible, awful, painful case. So what do I tell my innocent bride-to-be? Hey, sweetheart, sorry, but we're going to have to put off our wedding for a few weeks. I have been struck down again by a dreaded disease called gonorrhea. How did you catch that, Honey Jonas?

Well, sweetheart, I got it off a toilet seat when I served in a foreign land for the United States Marine Corps. Yeah, sure. Well, as you can see, I had a problem. And it was Hemingway My Hero who saved me. You ever read a Hemingway novel called *The Sun Also Rises?*"

"No, I don't think so. I read the one about the shark and the fisherman. . . ."

"It's about a guy named Jake who loses his virility—his balls—in a war. I told Helen, that's my wife, that I had had a Jake kind of injury in the Marines. She was an English teacher and talking Hemingway was what first made us interested in each other. So she knew what I meant. I told her that we were in luck, though, because unlike Jake's injury mine was curable. It would just take a few weeks. All it meant was that we had to delay consummating our marriage for a while. There had been no problem before, because those were the days when consummating was done mostly after the marriage. She bought it. At least she said she did. In other words, I got away with it. Terrible story, isn't it? I shouldn't have told you."

"I'll keep your secret."

"That's not the point. . . ."

I saw Thornton stumble a step. Then another. I reached forward for him. But I couldn't get a hold. He fell forward on his face.

Like a stick man that had been tipped over.

Jensen and I were down there with him immediately. So were the others. We turned him over. There was blood running out of his nose from where he had banged it when he fell on the blacktop road. His eyes were closed, his skin was almost white. Moisture was pouring down from his hair like a faucet of sweat had been turned on. Both of his hands were gripping his chest. His mouth was moving, but there was no sound.

I had seen the same thing happening to a man once before in my life. It was his heart. Thornton, the SSO Man from Pawnee City, Oklahoma, was having a heart attack. I knew it. They all knew it.

Jensen pushed me aside. Silently, like a paramedic in an instructional film, he began systematically, rhythmically pounding on Thornton's chest, blowing into his mouth.

Preacher said to Luther: "I'll stop a vehicle."

Luther said to Runyan: "Blankets. Get the blankets."

"He's still breathing," I said.

"Pulse?" Luther said, taking Thornton's right hand.

After a few seconds he said, "Yes. Barely."

All of our words were spoken in a businesslike hush. The way doctors and nurses probably talk in operating rooms, air traffic controllers in control towers, preachers in vestries, scientists in labs, mechanics under car hoods.

My eye went from watching the agony of Thornton trying to stay alive, to the road where Preacher was trying without success to flag down a car or a truck or something. Runyan must have been watching, too. Without saying a word to Preacher or anyone, he went out to the center of the road and started waving his arms. A small red panel truck, like the kind appliance repairmen and housepainters in Oklahoma use, was coming right at him. The driver braked and the truck began to slide, and finally it stopped before running over Runyan.

Preacher went around to the driver's side, opened the door and started talking in French to the man behind the wheel. He pointed over to Jensen and us. The man shook his head. I heard the motor being gunned, and gears being shifted.

Preacher reached inside, grabbed the man by his neck, jerked him out of the cab and threw him down on the road. The man was as big as Preacher, if not bigger, but it didn't seem to matter. As quick as anything like that I had ever seen, Preacher had the man on his stomach, one arm pinned behind him. He was screaming in French. Preacher was saying nothing. But he was smiling the smile of a man doing something he thoroughly enjoyed.

"There's still pulse," Luther said.

Jensen had not stopped. The chest hit, the blowing in the mouth. Again and again. Almost like somebody was counting cadence. One-two-three-four. Again. One-two-three-four. Again and again.

"The truck," Luther said.

Jensen nodded.

Runyan was back over and down with us now. He took Thornton by his left shoulder. I grabbed the right. Luther and Jensen each took a leg.

Thornton's clothes were soaked. But I could feel the warmth of life underneath.

We carried Thornton to the rear of the truck. Runyan

threw open the back door and out came a lovely breeze of fresh dough and yeast. The truck was full of big wicker baskets of long loaves of French bread and little rolls they call *croissants,* pronounced "crwa-*sahnts.*" We pushed some of them aside and lay Thornton down in the center on a bed of bread.

Luther tried to take over the job of saving Thornton's life. But Jensen shook him off and began again. A pound on the chest, a blow in the mouth. Pound, blow. Pound, blow.

Preacher brought the driver over to the truck. He brought him with a hammerlock around his neck and right arm, which was held twisted up behind his back. Preacher pushed him into the driver's seat, said something in French and then went around and jumped into the front passenger seat.

To us in back, Preacher said: "Be ready to grab him around the neck if he acts up. I have told him we have a dying man and to drive us to a hospital. I think he understands and will cooperate. We will now find out."

The truck lurched off.

Runyan grabbed one of Thornton's wrists. "Pulse is almost gone," he said after a few seconds.

Jensen just kept pounding and blowing. Again. Again. Again.

Thornton's face was now the color of the paper they use to print newspapers. His eyes were open and surrounded by red rings.

I tore off a piece of bread from one of the loaves. Then

I ripped it into two smaller pieces. And then into even smaller ones. Until I had a handful of mostly crumbs.

Pound. Blow. Pound. Blow.

Runyan grabbed a *croissant* and chewed and swallowed it in about three seconds.

Luther scooted up right behind the driver. He said something in French.

"Here comes a town," Preacher said. "I think he's playing it straight." He screamed something in French at the driver.

"Pulse gone," Runyan said softly to Jensen.

Jensen's face was now as red as catsup. I had the awful feeling he could have a heart attack, too. Right now. Right this very second. But he kept pounding and blowing.

"Here it is!" Preacher yelled.

In a few seconds there was the sound of the truck's brakes screeching, and we were stopped.

We flung open the truck door. Jensen, Runyan, Luther and I grabbed Thornton and lifted him up off the bread and out. My eye was caught by the bread underneath him. It was sopping wet from his sweat. It reminded me of the week-old bread we would put out for birds in Kansas. Sometimes the rain got it before the birds did, but the birds didn't mind. They still ate it.

Soon Preacher and a couple of women in white uniforms were there with a stretcher on wheels. We lay Thornton down in it, and they rolled him off toward a double door. The word "Urgences" was painted in red above it.

The driver of the truck was now screaming at us. And considering what we had done to his bread and croissants, I couldn't blame him. Luther went over and talked to him, and eventually pulled out a wad of French francs and handed them to the driver. The man, who was about fifty and was dressed in a blue kind of work clothes, looked at the bills, counted them and then took Luther's right hand and shook it. *"Merci, merci,"* he said several times. *Merci* means "thank you" in French.

He drove away and the rest of us walked toward the double doors.

"How much did you give him?" Runyan asked Luther.

"Less than a great Marine hero's life is worth," Luther replied.

8
· · ·
THE HYMN

WE FOUND a small waiting room with nobody in it. There were three white plastic chairs, a round red wooden table and several French magazines and newspapers strewn about. Jensen, who had come fully alive again, took one of the chairs. Runyan sat down in another. Preacher went to the bathroom, which he and the others called The Head. Luther stayed there at the door. So did I.

Runyan started babbling to Jensen. "Remember when that black kid in Weapons Company tripped with a flamethrower going full blast? His finger froze on the trigger and that burning juice sprayed up on him. It turned his skin and his uniform into white goo. We were on a landing with the Chinese marines down there in the southern part of Taiwan, Formosa, whatever it was called. The landing had a name—Operation Red Scare or something. Scare the Red Chinese into being good. There were fifteen hundred of us in the landing, nine hundred million of them. The kid was a corporal. From somewhere in Florida, I think. We all threw blankets on him and ran with him out of there to a truck, trying to get him to a hospital to save his life. It was a hospital like this. Remember how white he looked? I never figured out why the burning made him white. Somebody said something to him about going back to Florida white. Trying to be funny to cheer him up. But he didn't laugh or say anything. He was unconscious by then, and later he died. Jimmy Nolan from Worcester, Massachusetts—remember, he pronounced it like it's 'Wooster,' like in 'rooster'—was his platoon leader. Jimmy had to write the kid's family about how he died. Jimmy knew you were going to be a newspaper reporter, so he asked you to help him write the letter. I had to write a lot of those myself in Vietnam. . . ."

Luther drifted away, and I followed him. We headed together down the hall toward the emergency room but stopped after only a few steps.

"You do realize Thornton's dead, don't you, Luther?" I said in a voice just above a whisper.

"Have you ever seen anything like what Jonas did to save him?" he said. He was smiling. "Everybody was great. Everybody. Training and character pay off. Training and character. Have you ever seen reactions like that? Everybody moved. Everybody did their jobs."

"Sarah Thornton has probably already arrived back at

La Napoule. I hope you are thinking of what to say to her."

"I will say he died a hero. Sarah will be so pleased."

"Pleased her husband is dead? Come on, Luther...."

"We'll carry him out."

"Carry him out?"

"Marines carry out their dead and wounded. We'll carry him out." He was still smiling. Like he knew something nobody else knew. Like he was a madman of some kind. He was not looking at me. He was looking down the hall and out the door and far, far away, even from France.

"Luther, this is awful."

"No, it isn't," he said out the door and far, far away. "This is what we knew it might be like. People die."

"Luther, for God's sake, look at me! This is not war! This is a hike in France!"

"Same thing, Mack. Same, same, same. There are always casualties. Always." He did not look at me.

He turned around. "We'll bury him here. Where he died. Full military honors."

I followed him back toward the waiting room.

Runyan, the passed-over career Marine, was still talking. I had the feeling he had not stopped since we left. Preacher Hancock had returned from The Head.

Runyan said to everyone: "I never was able to figure out what to say to people after the death of somebody they loved. I couldn't in letters from Vietnam, I can't now even around our town. I live in a little town outside Baltimore. Aberdeen. Or I did before I ran away with you guys. A week or so before I left, I went to the funeral of a guy down the street who died of lung cancer. He was a big smoker and there was no surprise, because he'd been sick for months. But when it happened, I still could not think of anything to say to his wife. I said something like, 'Well, Diane, I wish it hadn't happened.' Stupid, really stupid. I'm already hoping I never run into any of Bobby's kin. Did I hear somebody say his wife was on her way over here? God, I hope not. . . ."

· · ·

They laid Thornton out on a cot in a private room so we could go in and see that he was dead. It was only the second time I had ever looked right into the face of a dead person. The first was Buck Vermillion, the driver of the Red River bus. I had been to a lot of open-casket funerals before that, but the deceased was always all made up to keep it from looking dead. In Oklahoma they even put rouge and lipstick on the men.

Thornton looked just like Buck. His skin was yellow like uncooked chicken. There were deep blue rings under his closed eyes. His thin black hair was wet and uncombed. There was no sign of a grin, a frown or any emotion in his lips, nose, chin or forehead.

And he was thinner. Like thirty pounds of weight had been sucked out of his body along with his life.

Runyan and I were on one side of the cot with Preacher. Jensen was on the other with Luther. All of them stood with their shoulders back, their stomachs in, their hands down by their sides. Without thinking, I did the same thing.

"Shall we bow our heads, please," Preacher said. Then, in a deep, dignified bellow, he prayed:

"Dear God of us all, take the spirit of our brother and do it proud. Take him to a life better than the one he had here. A life where there is glory and recognition, appreciation and honor for the quiet and the steady. A life where there is real forgiveness and mercy, where people love and cherish, where the wind is always warm and the sun always cool, where the spirit is alive and the flesh is dead rather than the other way around. Where dear Bobby Thornton can again be in command. In Your name we pray. Amen."

"The Hymn. Let's sing The Hymn," Runyan said.

The Hymn?

Standing very much erect, the four of them sang:

> "From the halls of Montezuma,
> To the shores of Tripoli;
> We fight our country's battles
> In the air, on land and sea;
> First to fight for right and freedom
> And to keep our honor clean,
> We are proud to claim the title of
> United States Marine. . . ."

Oh, yes. *That* hymn. We all learned to sing it in school during the war, along with the other service songs.

I kept my eye on Thornton while they sang. And thought about the nympho preacher's stupid prayer.

However bad Thornton's life was, it could not have

been worse than what it was now. Which was over. I had been listening to preachers in Kansas and Texas and Oklahoma tell people about the joys of the Hereafter for years and I had never believed a word of any of it. And I did not believe it now.

Baloney sounds the same wherever you hear it. Even in some little hospital in some little town in France with four crazy old men singing the Marines' Hymn over the body of the dead manager of a Sooner State Optical store in Pawnee City, Oklahoma.

. . .

They would not let us have Thornton. There was a thin little French doctor of about forty in a blond crew cut who talked quickly and in a high-pitched boy's choir voice about the laws of France that prevented people from walking into hospitals and carting off dead bodies. Even American dead bodies. Even when the would-be takers were good friends and former U.S. Marine comrades-in-arms of the dead man. Although the doctor spoke and understood English, he forced Luther and Preacher to do some of their pleading and arguing in French. But the rest of us had no trouble following what was going on.

Bodies of deceased people are released only to proven next-of-kin or to an accredited mortician, called an *entrepreneur des pompes funèbres,* pronounced "on-tre-preh-*noor* deh pomp foo-*nehbr*'," in French. The Republic of France makes no exceptions. Never ever. Good day, gentlemen.

So we hired an M. Rousseau to get Thornton's remains

out of the hospital. M. stood for "Monsieur." "Rousseau" was pronounced "roo-*sew*." He was an *entrepreneur des pompes funèbres*. His place of business was conveniently located only three blocks from the hospital. It was a two-story white frame house that was also his place of residence. He lived with his wife and two small daughters on the second floor. Parlors for viewing and weeping over the dead were on the first floor. The embalming and the other body preparation work were done in the basement.

M. Rousseau, a fat dark man around thirty-five, collected Thornton in a highly polished ancient black hearse that shone like a mirror in the moonlight. He drove it the three blocks at a dramatically sad two miles per hour with the five of us walking behind in a loose, mournful formation. Like a funeral procession.

I was surprised we were not made to sing The Hymn. Or one of their dirty marching songs about burying Marines under Russian whores or something.

While M. Rousseau worked in the basement making Thornton ready for departure to the Hereafter, we had a meeting of the minds in a first-floor parlor.

"I think we should carry him back to La Napoule," Preacher said, "the same way he got here."

"Let's think about that for a minute," Runyan said. "Let's think about how heavy those caskets are."

"It's the right thing to do, no question," Jensen said. "But not very practical. I'm not sure he would keep, for one thing. To be even more very practical about it."

Jonas Jensen, Kansas City newspaperman, was almost

a new person. Beating on Thornton's chest and blowing in his mouth had not saved Thornton, but it had done wonders for Jensen. His face was still round and his stomach was still a balloon, but the pink-eyed stare of the forlorn and lost was gone. There was a grin in the eyes and on the mouth, and the sound of life and Hemingway had returned to his voice.

"We must carry him out," Luther said, like nobody had yet spoken. "That is our obligation. That is our duty."

We were all sitting in flowered chairs and couches. Preacher now stood up. As if pronouncing the Word of God, he said: "Then it's decided. We'll march with one of us at each corner of the casket, like pallbearers do at funerals. That leaves one of us always in reserve. We will rotate around the casket every thirty minutes, with one dropping out to rest. We will also break every thirty minutes instead of fifty. It will be difficult, but it can be done.

"As they said at Basic School, the difficult will be done immediately. The impossible will take a little longer."

"Hear, hear," Runyan said.

"Okay," Jensen said. "Aye, aye."

I had suddenly had it with these people. I jumped to my feet. And turned to Luther, my friend, and speaker of the Oklahoma House of Representatives.

"No! Count me out. There will be no fifth in reserve. This is insane, Luther. Absolutely, one hundred percent, Boomer Sooner nuts. One man is already dead. For what did he die? So you all could relive something out of your pasts that never existed. What have you accomplished? Nothing but murder. What have you proven? What does carrying a casket down some blacktop roads in France until another of you collapses and dies, maybe, prove? It proves insanity. Stupidity."

Luther kept a half-grin on his face while I talked. One of those sicky, superior grins. Now he turned away from me to the others and said in his steady voice, "Saddle up!"

And they strutted single file like fools out of the parlor. Luther first, then Runyan, Jensen and Preacher.

"F—— you!" I screamed at the top of my lungs. "F—— all of you!"

It was the first time I had actually used that awful word. Out loud.

I felt like a fool. An unclean fool. And I hoped that M. Rousseau's wife and daughters up on the second floor did not hear me.

9

. . .

AHHHH-EEEE!

SARAH THORNTON did not cry when I told her that her husband was dead. She screamed. She screamed at the top of her lungs like she had been stabbed. The scream was not a word. Just the sound of Ahhhhh-eeeee! Ahhhh-eeee! Ahhhhh-eeee!

I had come back to La Napoule on a night bus, a French-made luxury coach with huge windows. It was a very impressive bus, even though the seats did not recline like they had on Buck Vermillion's Trailways Silver Eagle. The driver also was no Buck. He looked worse alive than Buck did dead. No uniform, no hat. He needed a shave and some manners. He was no piece for our bus museum.

The trip took four hours, which seemed incredible when I realized how long it took for us to march it.

Sarah Thornton was in the lobby of the Hôtel La Liberté. It was six in the morning and she was sitting wide awake in an overstuffed chair. She resembled her sister back at the SSO: plump, unattractive, friendly, afraid. I took her into a writing room off to one side. After first asking about her flight over from Oklahoma City and other small matters, I told her.

When the Ahhh-eeee screaming stopped, she asked: "Who killed him?"

"Nobody really. He killed himself."

"Bob was no suicide."

So I told her the whole story. I told her what I had been told had happened in Kansas City. The decision to run away and try to be Marines again. The march. The blisters. The collapse. The heroic effort to save him.

"Where is he now?" she asked. She looked around and behind me, thinking maybe I had him with me. Maybe in a suitcase? Had I left him on the bus?

"They are marching back here with him. Carrying him along the road."

"In a casket?"

"Yes, ma'am."

"That's crazy!"

"Yes, ma'am."

"He'll die again!"

She screamed again. Ahhhhh-eeeee! Ahhhhh-eeeee!

I had no choice but to go with her in search of a vehicle we could use to locate and rescue her late husband's remains.

.   .   .

We found a service station that rented cars and took American Express. I got a special station wagon so we would have room to haul the casket. The one they gave me was made by a French company called Peugeot, pronounced, "poo-*zhow*." I had seen a few before but not many. Volkswagens, Volvos and Mercedes-Benzes were the main European cars in Oklahoma.

Sarah Thornton jabbered while we rode out of town in search of her dead husband and his friends.

She jabbered about how Bobby should have been promoted to regional vice-president of Sooner State Optical and probably would have if he had gone to OU instead of South Central Oklahoma State, and if instead of being a Methodist he had been a Baptist like the executive vice-president and general manager of SSO. And if he had had more of a flair for numbers and if he could have worked up real enthusiasm for glasses and contact lenses when he talked about them to the customers and to the other employees at SSO. She said Bobby just never saw any excitement in optical work. He always said that half of the people who bought glasses didn't really need them, anyhow. That was a bad attitude for somebody in the business, and the people at the top of SSO knew it. He talked a lot about buying a truck stop out on I-35. He said at least that would bring to his life the excitement of being around trucks and drivers and highway patrolmen with stories and troubles.

She jabbered on about how she and Bobby had met: They were both students at South Central and they had the same last name, Thornton. They weren't related, and they even came from different parts of the state. She was

from Enid, he was from Duncan. They happened to take
the same big freshman lecture course on comparative religion, where seating was alphabetical, and there they
were, sitting side by side on the last row. Robert Wilson
Thornton of Duncan and Sarah Louise Thornton of Enid.
After a while they were friendly, and by the end of the
semester they were dating, which they did steadily and
without interruption through all four years of college.
Bobby had been in Navy ROTC and took what was called
the Marine Option. He was commissioned a second lieutenant in the Marines at a ceremony an hour after they
had both gotten their college diplomas. The next weekend they were married at her home Methodist church in
Enid.

She jabbered:

"It's been no fun living with this thing of my maiden
name also being my married name. Nobody believes it's
so, is the main thing. I have had damn fool bankers and
damn fool people at the courthouse and lots of other damn
fools look at me like I didn't know my own real name.
Like I was demented or retarded. 'Your maiden name,
Mrs. Thornton?' 'Thornton.' 'No, ma'am. That's your
married name. I meant your maiden name. The one
you had before you married.' 'I know what a maiden
name is. Mine is Thornton. I am the daughter of Ralph
and Louise Peggy Thornton of Enid, Oklahoma. If you
do not believe it then you can go straight to H-E-L-L.'
It has not been easy, Mr. Lieutenant Governor. Not easy
at all. Do you have any daughters, Mr. Lieutenant Governor?"

"Call me Mack," I said. "Yes, I have two daughters."

"Well, tell them to for God's sake stay away from men and boys who have the same last name as theirs. There is H-E-L-L down that road. Look what's happened to me. Here I am in this godforsaken foreign country trying to find my husband, and lo and behold, he died. Can you imagine dying somewhere other than Oklahoma? I can't. I was with Bobby when he was in the Marines in California before he went overseas. California is just like this place. Hot, stupid, strange. I am glad you have children. We don't have any. There's something wrong with my insides that made it impossible. Neither of us wanted to adopt. Well, I might have, but Bobby was the one who really didn't want to. He said there was no way you could tell how they would grow up. It's probably just as well now. It's only me who's going to cry at his funeral. If we had children there, they'd be crying their eyes out. Thank God for some things. There's so much not to thank Him for. Thank Him for those he does deserve."

And before long there they were. Four men and a casket, moving ever so slowly down the shoulder of the road. The casket was that grayish-brown metallic color so popular for Volvos and other foreign cars. Luther and Runyan were on the front corners, Preacher and Jensen on the rear two. Each had a hand on one of the side pallbearers' carry handles. Each had a strained look on his face. Even Preacher and Luther.

I pulled the Peugeot over to the left side of the road and braked to a stop right in front of them. Sarah Thornton jumped out before I had it fully stopped.

"Put him down!" she screamed. "Put my Bobby down right this minute! Luther, you fool! Put him down!"

And she broke once again into her screech.

Ahhhhh-eeeee! Ahhhhh-eeeee!

They set the casket down. Luther came toward Sarah. "I am so sorry," he said. "I am so sorry about Bobby. He was good man. . . ."

"Open it," said Sarah, walking right past him to the casket.

"Open it?" Luther said.

"Open it."

Preacher said, "Now Mrs. Thornton, that would not be in the best interests of all concerned. It's also against the law. . . ."

I was there now. She turned to me. "Will you please open the casket, Mack? You are the lieutenant governor of Oklahoma, you can do anything you want."

I walked over, bent down and found a latch on one side of the casket. It was like a release on a car trunk. I pulled it. The lid popped loose. I lifted it up slowly on its hinges.

Bobby Thornton of Pawnee City, Oklahoma, was present and accounted for. He was still dead, of course, but his appearance was much improved over the last time I had seen him dead. His hair had been combed. There was color in his cheeks and the dark rings were gone from around his eyes. He was wearing a white dress shirt and a dark blue tie. They had even moved the corners of his lips into a smile.

Sarah Thornton went down on her knees and looked over the casket rim at Bobby.

She broke into her Ahhhhh-eeeee scream.

Then she cried. And so did I. I could never keep from crying once somebody else started. Like laughing or throwing up.

It went on for more than twenty minutes while she sobbed and caressed Bobby's face like it was an expensive vase. After a while his cheeks and chin were glistening from the wet of her pouring tears.

The only thing like it I had ever seen was what my sister, Meg, did when our mother died of a burst appendix. I was twelve and Meg was fourteen. She cried and howled like a little animal for hours and hours with sounds that pierced my skin and made me shiver.

Sarah Thornton Thornton made me wonder how Jackie would—will—react when I die. Is there a connection between love in life and tears in death?

Preacher Hancock, the professional handler of grief, had gotten down on his knees and stayed down there with Sarah Thornton. Occasionally he would say something I could not hear. And he patted her on the shoulder or took her hands.

Finally it stopped, and she was silent. I leaned down and suggested that maybe we should close the lid now and take Bobby back to Oklahoma.

Luther made the mistake of also leaning down. He said: "He died a hero, Sarah."

She leapt to her feet and pushed him away like he was garbage.

"You fool," she said in a quiet firm voice. "You *idiot* fool. Bobby was no hero. He just wanted to be somebody that mattered again, like he was when he was a Marine. You stayed being somebody. The speaker of the House. Bobby was so proud of you. You should have known better. You killed my Bobby."

"He had a heart attack. He died a Marine. . . ."

"You fool." Then to me, "Mack, get me and my Bobby as far away from this fool and this foreign fool place as you can. As fast as you can."

.   .   .

I drove the station wagon and she rode in the back with the casket. I had folded down the backseat to get the casket in, which meant she had to sit cross-legged on the floor. It was not the best position.

Preacher and Runyan offered to go with us, but she declined their offer with a contemptuous shake of her head. Her screaming, sobbing sadness had turned to hate.

She started jabbering the second the doors were closed and we were moving.

"They should all be tried for murder. They killed my Bobby as sure as if they had shot him in the heart with a twenty-two rifle. Running away from home like little boys, and then like idiot fools going on a hike in France like they were big tough Marines again. They knew at their age that somebody would die. Somebody *had* to die. It wouldn't have counted and wouldn't have been worth it and real if there weren't any casualties. 'Casualties'— that's a great Marine word. Bobby and them used to use it a lot back in the fifties, but they never had any because nobody ever got hurt doing what they were doing. Which was mostly drinking and hiking. Now they have one. A real casualty. Think of what Luther and those other fools now have to talk about at their next reunion. Remember that time we walked around France until Bobby Thornton dropped dead? God, what a time that was. Remember how his crazy wife came and cried and cried over his body. Remember? God, how exciting. God, what a great, grown-up time that was. Wow-ee, wow.

"I do not get Luther. Born rich and smart, went north to college, married good. An Oklahoma hero all his life. Big shot there with you and the others in Oklahoma City. Name in the paper all of the time. On TV a lot. Bobby just loved knowing he knew him. Everybody in Pawnee City knew Bobby had been a Marine with Luther Wallace. *Everybody*. What in the world did Luther have to run away from? Bobby's life didn't work for him after the Marines. I saw it not working. I was there. I saw every second of it not working. But Luther? His life worked like a charm. What in Jesus God's name is he doing running away? The man's a fool. It's one thing not to have anything, like Bobby, but it's worse to have it, like Luther, and not have the sense to know you have it. What do you think, Mack?"

"I agree."

"With what?"

"That Luther is worse."

"Is he really a friend of yours?"

"Yes. We always got along. You're right about his being smart. *The Daily Oklahoman* said he was the smartest man in state government."

"Then why did he do what he did?"

"He says it was because he was tired of being responsible."

"Now that really is stupid. He really is a fool. All my Bobby wanted was to *be* responsible again."

· · ·

It took a while, but we found a funeral director in La Napoule who spoke enough English to understand we needed help with a dead man we had in the back of a station wagon. We needed him shipped air express to Pawnee City, Oklahoma, USA. The mortician was named Chevalier, like the movie star. Paul Chevalier. He had spent six weeks in St. Paul, Minnesota, on an exchange program twenty years before, when he was in high school. He was extremely nice and accommodating but he said it would take a while. Two days, maybe more. There were papers that had to be filled out, back in the town where Bobby had died. There were releases and permissions to be obtained, and rules to be observed. He said the French were strict on allowing dead bodies shipped out of their country, and Americans were difficult and picky in allowing bodies shipped into theirs. He took an imprint of my American Express card, and Sarah Thornton and I went off to the Hôtel La Liberté to wait two days, maybe more.

The first thing I did after settling in at the hotel was to call C. in Oklahoma City.

I told him about the death of Bobby Thornton and what we were doing to bring the body back. I also asked him to tell Annabel Wallace that the trip was costing more than expected because of that.

"Anything new to tell her about Luther?" C. asked.

"No. He's still cuckoo. Getting worse every day. Tell her not to expect him back. Ever."

"Ever?"

"Right."

I told C. to give Jackie and Janice Alice a call to bring them up to date on what was going on and when I would probably be home.

"Anything happened there in Oklahoma?" I asked C., just making conversation.

"Big news here is still The Chip's new idea for the turnpikes. He's got 'em on the run, saying in the papers that he sure hopes the legislature doesn't vote against The Mick and Nita. Particularly since both of them are still alive and would be humiliated so much in public all over America and the world. The guy's the smartest stupid man I've ever known."

"Am I being missed by the people of Oklahoma?"

"I don't think anybody but me has noticed yet you're gone."

I came within a hair of saying to him what I said to Luther and the boys when they decided to walk back to La Napoule with Bobby Thornton in the casket. It was scary how close I came to saying it again. Just like that. Right over a transatlantic phone line right into Oklahoma.

What I said instead was, "Oh, thank you, sir."

Then he said, "You don't happen to have a bishop there in your group, do you?"

"No, why?"

"The Methodist bishop of North Carolina has turned up missing. I saw a national Missing Persons bulletin on him the other day. I've got the report on it right here in front of me. It says he had been a Marine officer in the late fifties. He's not on that reunion list we got from Annabel, but I thought there could still be a connection."

"Where in North Carolina did he live?"

"Raleigh, it says. Went away to the airport to go to a bishops' meeting in Miami and never showed up there."

"What's his last name?"

"Hancock."

"Well, well, well. We do indeed have the missing bishop. He's the nympho I was telling you about."

"Hey, Mack, good-bye. Your sense of humor has gone French or worse."

"Hey, C., good-bye to you. Yours has always been French or worse. Seriously. He's here."

"Doing what?"

"Same thing as Luther. Being stupid and crazy playing Marine."

"I'll notify the people in Raleigh."

"Sure," I said without thinking. And then after a beat of thought, I said: "No, C. Don't do that. Not yet."

"Why not? Those Methodists are probably worried sick down there."

"I don't know. It just doesn't seem right."

"Hey, Mack, Luther and his Marine loonies aren't getting to you, are they?"

"No, sir. No way."

Not unless you counted talking filthy for the first time in my life.

It was only then that I thought of Buck Vermillion and the Red River bus. It was amazing how it had sailed almost completely out of my mind. I asked C. if there was anything new.

"Still nothing. I did carry out my assignment. That schedule had five or six regulars. Most of them were on the bus and died with it."

"But somebody wasn't?"

"One guy. He was down with the flu. It saved his life."

"Have you talked to him?"

"About what, Mack?"

"I don't know. What it was like on that bus, I guess."

"Sure, Mack. Why don't you ask him when you get back? So long for now."

"Sure, C."

10

...

SAME TO YOU, MR. SPEAKER

THE LOONIES of One-Nine showed up at the Hôtel La Liberté that evening. They had not had time to march it, so I figured they had taken the bus. Or rented a car. Or hitchhiked. Or sprouted wings like crazy people in fairy tales and flown back to La Napoule.

I knew they were back, because I ran into Runyan in the lobby. We smiled but said nothing to each other. I hadn't known him when I arrived in France, and I would leave not knowing him. We had nothing in common besides the death of Bobby Thornton of Pawnee City, Oklahoma. Passed over for promotion? Why? He was a strange man who would be a permanent stranger to me. But I had no trouble understanding why he had run away to France.

I felt the same way about Jonas Jensen. He wasn't like

most of the newspapermen I knew in Oklahoma. The guys at home were mostly normal people who were happy with where they lived and what they were doing. Jensen, like Bobby Thornton, felt passed over for life. Thumping on and puffing into Thornton was probably the most important thing he had done in twenty-five years.

Luther and Preacher were the two who made no sense at all. As Sarah Thornton said, the worst thing of all is to have it made and not know it.

Luther left a note for me at the desk. He said he would like to talk to me before I left for home. I wasn't sure whether I wanted to talk to him. I had all I wanted, all I needed, of Luther Dean Wallace. I would go back to Oklahoma City and report to Annabel that her husband no longer knew the difference between right and wrong, as the courthouse lawyers put it. I would tell her not to expect him back but if he ever did return it would probably be as a different person. The man who had been speaker of the Oklahoma House of Representatives was gone and probably gone forever.

Preacher Hancock, the Methodist nympho, was a different situation. I *did* want to talk to him. Mostly just to let him know that I did not appreciate his cute little lies about his sex obsession problems and that I had been skeptical from the beginning. But also, for some weird reason I felt I needed his permission to let the Methodists of North Carolina know of his whereabouts. And I was curious about why he had run away.

I saw Preacher the next morning at the village dime-store place. I had gone there to pick up some toothpaste. The tube of Crest I had brought with me had been down to its last dozen squirts when I'd left Oklahoma, and I had just rolled it up to its final gasp. Preacher was looking through a table of white T-shirts with a big-finned fish and "La Napoule" emblazoned on the front in light blue and pink. They were tacky, like the kind high school kids at home buy at county fairs.

I saw him first, so I had the element of surprise. "Hi there, Most Reverend Bishop," I said.

Preacher smiled. "So you know."

"So I know. So you must think you were pretty funny with that nymphomaniac story."

"Yes, as a matter of fact." The smile was still there. He was totally unconcerned. He held the shirt up to his chest. "What do you think?"

"Hardly the kind of thing you'd expect to see on the Methodist bishop of North Carolina."

"True." He handed a clerk some French paper money and then put the shirt on over the regular short-sleeved shirt he was already wearing. "How do I look now, Mack?"

"Nutty."

"Good," he said.

We walked outside to the street together. He turned toward the beach and I stayed with him. In a few minutes, we were down where we had played kick-the-can. We went to the rock where we had talked the other morning, and sat down.

"Why did I lie about who I was, is what you would like to know," he said. These were the first words either of us had spoken since we left the store. "Frankly, it made it easier to explain why I was here. I was running away from failure. It's a natural two-plus-two-equals-four. Bishops don't run away."

"Neither do House speakers."

"True."

"Luther keeps telling me he just got tired of being responsible. That's why he's here. Please don't give me that same line. Please."

"You can't handle the truth, huh, Mack?"

"Preacher, look . . . what is your real first name?"

"Morris. My fellow bishops call me Moe. Everybody else calls me Bishop or Reverend. Reverend is my real first name. Hi, Reverend. Have another piece of home-made chocolate pecan fudge, Reverend. Will you preside at my wedding, Reverend? Will you bury my husband, Reverend? Will you give the invocation at next week's Rotary, Reverend? Please pass the mashed potatoes and gravy, Reverend. I love that new red tie, Reverend. Would you mind talking to my son about masturbating, Reverend? Can we count on you to speak to the Ecumenical Dinner again this year, Reverend? How about being chairman of the local chapter of the National Conference of Christians and Jews this year, Reverend? Do you bless new cars, Reverend? How about motorcycles, Reverend? Boats, Reverend? Would you be interested in coming deer hunting with six or seven of us, Reverend? Tell me again why it's a sin to drink a Bud every once in a while, Reverend. . . ."

"Okay, okay, I get it, I get it," I said. I didn't really get it, but I also had no interest in arguing with him about it. Like Luther, he had come up with an explanation that didn't explain anything.

He asked me if I had children. I said yes. Grandchildren? No, I said.

Then, in a most dramatic form of his pulpit voice, he told me a story that haunts me to this day. He said:

"You don't follow it, Mack. I know that and I don't blame you. Let me tell you what even Luther and the others do not know. The reason I am here, the real reason I am here, Mack, is because of a grandchild. My only grandchild. A little boy two years and three months old. Son of our daughter Joanna and her husband, Wayne. One great little boy. Named Moe for me. Everybody called him Moe Two. I adored him. I loved his smells and his sounds. I loved everything about him. They said—everybody said—he was my spit and image, and he was. They lived in Charleston. Charleston, South Carolina. They came up often, particularly on holidays like Thanksgiving. On Thanksgiving Day of last year, I took little Moe Two with me to bless the Thanksgiving dinner at a shelter for the homeless and forlorn in Raleigh. I had been doing it every Thanksgiving for years. Little Moe Two was in the front seat with me. The shelter was only ten blocks or so from our house, so I did not make him sit in back or fasten a seat belt. He loved to listen to the radio. I had it on very loud. I drove into the intersection at Sixth and Blount just as a fire truck, a big one, came from the other direction. I had not heard the siren and had not seen the truck. It hit us broadside on Moe Two's side. He was thrown through the windshield of the car and out onto the pavement. It happened so fast I couldn't even move to grab him. I had my belt on. I was not even scratched. His little body was smashed to ribbons and he died right there on the street at Sixth and Blount.

"My wife and my daughter and my son-in-law were torn to ribbons by little Moe's death. They needed comforting, something they had always gotten from me, The Great Comforter. Reverend Moe the Rock, the Marine bishop. It was simply the most terrible thing one could imagine. They and everybody else I loved were devastated by what it had also done to me. They comforted me with words about how I of all persons should and could understand how these kinds of tragedies happen to the most undeserving people. After all, I had spent my life being strong in the face of tragedy—other people's tragedy. Helping people get through what I was going through was what God had called me to do. And nobody, but nobody, did it better. The Rock. That was what I was. The man everybody wanted next to them when something like this happened to them. Thank God, they said, thank God I knew what to do for myself. Thank God.

"Well, Mack, I did not know what to do for myself. Or for my brokenhearted wife and daughter and son-in-law. I did not know what to do for anybody.

"So when I called Jonas to say I was sorry I hadn't made it to the Kansas City reunion and he mentioned something about running away to France, I said, Yes, sir, good idea, when do we leave? I'm sorry about the nympho story. I just didn't want any questions. This trip was clearly for failures. How could the bishop of North Carolina be considered a failure?"

I wanted to reach out and comfort this big man. I wanted to make him believe it was all right. But I knew it would never ever be all right for him. Ever again.

"I am so sorry, Moe," was all I could say.

"I told you about Moe Two not so you would be sorry, but so you wouldn't think me to be a complete fool—to use Sarah Thornton's word. Even as an irresponsible run-away, there's still something in me that wants to be liked and respected. It's too late to completely turn that off, I guess. Part of me will always be the successful Methodist bishop of North Carolina."

"Do you want to be found?"

"No. Not yet."

"You can't stay here forever, can you? Isn't it too late for that, too?"

"Have a good trip back to Oklahoma, Mack. I am so sorry about Bobby Thornton."

"So am I."

·   ·   ·

I was stunned almost sick by Moe Hancock's story. I wanted to scream at somebody in charge. I wanted to apologize for all the times I had felt sorry myself. When my mother died. When I lost my left eye. When Pepper died in Korea. I tried to imagine how I would have handled such an awful thing as Moe's. I couldn't imagine it. None of it. What must it have been like for Moe to look down on that pavement and see his dead little grandson? What *must* that have been like? How could anybody recover from such a thing? Ever?

I could not think of anything more to say to Moe. Nothing. After several long minutes of silence, I asked if he wanted to go get some coffee or breakfast or a drink or anything at all anywhere. Anywhere in the world. No, thank you, he said. He would just walk the beach for a while. So I left him and headed back toward the hotel. But I didn't want to go there. I decided to go over to the museum to see the Gauguin stuff again. I figured it would take my mind off of little Moe Two on the pavement at Sixth and Blount in Raleigh, North Carolina, if nothing else.

Luther was in the museum. He was standing in front of a painting called *Matamoe*. I remembered it from my first visit. I had no idea what a matamoe was, if anything. The explanation plaque next to it didn't explain it, of course. Explanations of things seldom explain things. The painting was pretty big, about three feet wide and four feet tall. It was a scene from an island jungle, as were so many of Gauguin's pictures. The sky was yellow and the trees and grass were deep green. There was lots of orange in lagoons and plants. Up front were a peacock and a smaller bird, plus a native guy in a purple swimsuit cutting wood. Barely visible in the background were two women in colorful long dresses. It was hard to tell if they were walking toward the woodcutter and the peacock or away from them.

"Tell me, Mr. Speaker, what is the true, deep, real, significant, important, cultural, artistic meaning of this lovely piece of art?" I said to Luther when I came up beside him.

Immediately and without looking at me, Luther said, "Mr. Lieutenant Governor, the meaning of art, like the meaning of a turnpike, is always in the eye of the beholder."

"How does it behold to you, Mr. Speaker?"

"Well, sir, I am sorry to say the message of this work is destruction. Destruction of the basic democratic two-house form of government in the State of Oklahoma as we now know it."

With Luther still not looking at me, I said, "It is amazing that a Frenchman who died of venereal disease when he was fifty-four was able to capture exactly that Oklahoma story on canvas like this. What is the significance of the peacock?"

"That's our friend the governor, watching and preening and doing nothing except dreaming of new turnpikes to build."

"The small bird?"

"The lieutenant governor, doing his best as always to preserve and·protect what is Sooner right, upright and proper."

"The woodcutter?"

"He is the spirit of corruption and decay."

"The two women?"

"The double temptations of loot and root."

"Loot and root?"

"Loot as in money, root as in screw."

I looked again at the placard on the wall. It said, *Matamoe* was there on loan from the Pushkin Museum of Fine Art in Moscow. I pointed to it and said, "The Russians are behind this."

"Precisely," he said. "They are behind everything." We were now facing each other.

" 'Precisely' is C.'s word."

"Have you talked to Oklahoma's fearless law enforcer lately?"

I told Luther there was still nothing new on the Red River bus tragedy and realized I had neglected to tell him anything about it. When I was through with the story, he shook his head. "Imagine what the last few miniseconds of life must have been like for those twenty-four people," he said. And that was all he said.

I started telling him about Buffalo Joe's idea of naming the turnpikes for The Mick and for Nita Pickens of Perkins Corner, but he stopped me by putting his hands up to his ears. "No, please. No. Thinking about what your friend Joe might do to Oklahoma is the only thing that might get me to come home," he said.

"You should know, Luther, that C. said they have already forgotten about both of us."

"I'm so sorry about you, Mack. I did not want that to

happen. Oklahoma needs to always remember you."

"You remember what you said to me a couple of times since I've been here, and what I yelled at you the other day when you left the hospital?"

"No, nothing in particular . . ."

"A charade clue for you, then, sir. It's two words. First word rhymes with . . ." I made like I was trying to shove a stuck car out of a ditch.

" 'Push'?"he said.

"Second word rhymes with . . ." I blew air out of my mouth.

" 'Blow.' First word rhymes with 'push,' second with 'blow.' Okay, now, what can that be?"

"When you in all of your wisdom and education do finally come up with it, consider it said to you now. At the top of my lungs."

He was smiling. So was I.

"Mr. Lieutenant Governor, I am still shocked from the other day. If the people of Oklahoma ever found out you used that kind of language they might . . . well, elect you governor."

He stuck out his right hand. I took it. What choice did I have? He still was my friend, insane and stupid as he had turned out to be. How could I be mad at a friend just because he had gone crazy?

"I'm glad you found me before you left," he said. "I just wanted to say good-bye."

"I didn't find you. I came in here on my own and you just happened to be here."

"I'll say good-bye anyway, if that's okay."

"Sure."

We shook each other's hand again with vigor.

"So you're staying?" I said.

"Yes, sir."

"Till when?"

"Till I feel like going home."

"You're going to miss being speaker."

"I know."

"You're going to miss these little games with me...."

"You still do not understand any of this, do you, Mack?"

"I understand the others. Even Preacher now. But not you. It's crazy for you."

"Crazy is the point. I have to be crazy for once in my life. Just this once. I have to."

"Sure thing, Mr. Speaker."

"F—— you, Mr. Lieutenant Governor."

"Same to you, Mr. Speaker."

• • •

It was good I was going back to Oklahoma.

I went all the way to Pawnee City with Sarah and the casket. Funeral-home people from there met our flight in Oklahoma City and took the three of us—Sarah, Bobby and me—the last hundred miles in two gray Cadillacs. A hearse for Bobby and a limo for Sarah and me following right behind down I-35.

It had been a terrible trip from France. Sarah was jabbering when we got on the Air France plane at Nice, she was still at it when we landed in New York, and she continued throughout the Braniff flights to Dallas and then on to Oklahoma City. At New York and Dallas, special airline people were there to help us, to make sure the casket in the baggage compartment and we in the passenger cabin got on and stayed on the same flights.

I don't remember much of what Sarah said, because I did my best to tune her out. The main thing that stuck in my memory is shoes. She talked about shoes a lot. A favorite uncle of hers had run a shoe store in Enid that was the Thom McAn affiliate for north central Oklahoma. She made it sound like being chosen by Thom McAn was like being selected for the U.S. Supreme Court. She explained the ratio between size and width, and what podiatrists, or foot doctors, suggested about tightness and looseness in the heel to avoid blisters. It was a strange thing to talk about under normal circumstances, but particularly so because of Bobby's blisters. I did not tell her about how he had cut off the backs of his cheap tennis shoes in order to keep walking until he died. I was sure she had seen enough of his dead body to know what bloody pulps blisters had made of his heels, so she was just talking. She said she wished she could have talked Bobby into going into shoes instead of glasses. She said it was a much more gentle and wholesome business. I did not ask her what that meant, because I did not care.

She did not sleep one minute from the time we left Nice until we pulled up to the Cochran Brothers Funeral Home in Pawnee City twenty-two and a half hours later. She did not remain silent for more than a few minutes during that time. She did not ask me one question about me or anything else. She just talked. And talked and talked. I am sorry to say it helped me understand even more why Bobby Thornton had run away to France. Clearly he'd had more than one reason.

Sarah Thornton would not let me leave Pawnee City until I promised to return in three days for Bobby's funeral. She wanted me to give a eulogy.

"I barely knew your husband," I said.

"Eulogies should be given by people who were with people when they actually died," she said.

I had never heard that before and it did not make sense, but I was too tired out and too tired of her to argue.

"Also, you saw him at his best," she added.

His best? Marching through little towns in France like a crazy man? Dying?

⋅ ⋅ ⋅

Buffalo Joe wanted to know only one thing. Was Luther coming back to resume being speaker of the House?

"Not anytime soon," I said.

"What does soon mean?" asked Joe. "At least a month?"

"Yeah, I think so."

"I have to know, Mack. I have to know for certain."

"Why, Joe?"

"Because of the turnpikes."

Then he told me what he had devised. It was what in my travel and emotional weariness seemed the most idiotic thing I had ever heard from Joe. There was already quite a list from the years we had served the people of the

Sooner State. Once he had promoted an effort finally to put a dome on our capital, the only state capitol building in the country without a dome. Oklahoma had run out of money for it when the building was being constructed just before World War I. He had had me and everybody else in the state going around saying "Crown Oklahoma" all the time. On another occasion, he had come back from a goodwill trip to Japan with a plan to sell off large underutilized and underloved sections of our state to the Japanese, on the grounds that the Japanese needed land, Oklahoma needed money, so why not solve each other's problem? He didn't really end up calling his plan "Sell Oklahoma," but that's what it amounted to. Fortunately, neither one of these plans came off.

Now, as I sat across the desk from him in his office at the capitol, he said:

"Haden and them have come with their hands up. They're ready to deal. But they've said, Pick one or the other. They will go for one but not for two. But that is a problem. We've got the folks from Sturant and down there pushing like hell for the Nita Pickens Turnpike, right? We've got the folks from up north pushing like hell for a Mickey Mantle Turnpike, right? How in the world can I or anyone else choose between those two great Sooner Citizens? I ask you, Mack, how could anyone choose between the two of them? Could you do it, Mr. Second Man?" Second Man of Oklahoma was what he sometimes called me. In private.

"No, sir," I said.

"Okay, so what do we people in the business of governing do when such situations arise? We compromise in a spirit of cooperation, that is what we do. So here's my idea. Instead of building just one four-lane turnpike, we build two two-lane turnpikes. That's all either is worth in the first place. We can do both for the price of one four-lane and everybody is happy. What do you think, Mack?"

Joe was from Buffalo, Oklahoma, up in the Panhandle. But as I explained earlier, he also had a buffalo's face and dark brown hair and he wore mostly dark brown suits, white shirts and black ties. In other words, it was almost uncanny that the nickname "Buffalo Joe" would have fit even if he had been from some place like Tulsa. Heaven forbid. But at this particular moment C.'s private nickname for him, "The Chip," as in buffalo chip, seemed even more appropriate.

I said: "It's a bad idea, Joe. A very bad idea. There are no such things as two-lane turnpikes. They'll laugh you out of the state. People will make jokes about it on national TV. People like Nita Pickens of Perkins Corner herself will write songs about two-lane turnpikes to nowhere."

Joe got up from his chair and came around toward me. He was not smiling. This meeting was over.

"You're wrong, Mack. Dead wrong. A two-lane turnpike is better than no turnpike at all. I will be admired once again statewide for my ability to make government work for the people."

I stood and, knowing my time was over, headed for the door.

"On second thought, you're probably right, Joe," I said as I arrived at his office door.

"Good thinking, Mack. France hasn't completely destroyed your mind. The only thing that could screw it up is Luther. He would raise so much public hell it wouldn't be worth it. I didn't want to make my idea public till you got back. I'm banking on your word he isn't coming back in time to kill this thing."

"Bank on it," I said.

By the time I was back around the hallway corner in my own office, I was a happy man. The governor had given me a very good idea for furthering the business of government by killing his stupid idea for two two-lane turnpikes.

. . .

Annabel Wallace treated me like what I was. A hired hand. I told her that Luther was in good health and that despite the Marine shenanigans and the fact that one of his companions had died, he was likely to remain in good health.

"Now as to the question of why he went there in the first place," I said. "My view is that he had a desire to change his life-style. He was tired of being who he was and doing what he had always done. It's hard to figure that being speaker wasn't enough, but who are we to explain what the mind does to a person? Even to somebody who has always been as level-headed and wonderful as

Luther. I think he just wanted to be something different. This Marine thing came along, so he took it. Someday I am sure he will communicate this directly to you, either by mail or on the phone."

I paused for Annabel to ask a question. Any comments? Any reaction at all?

None. Her eyes were two blanks. Like she was about to read a chart at the eye doctor's.

So I continued: "He spoke a lot about being irresponsible and crazy for a change. It was all dumb talk that makes no sense. How can a grown man with Luther's background and life suddenly decide he's tired of being responsible? It doesn't add up. But like I said, that's what he said."

Annabel Wallace, sitting across from C. and me in the same room and seats of our first two conversations, clearly could not have cared less. She glanced at her wristwatch, which was encircled in diamonds.

I went on with my report.

"For the record, I think it is well that you know that there is nothing of an illegal or illicit nature involved in his life there in France. He and his Marine buddies just eat and hike around. They also talk a lot about what it was like when they were all in the Marines together. Some of their stories are really quite funny. It must have been an important and interesting time in all of their lives, and they miss it. I could give you an example of the kinds of things they talk about, if you like."

"No, thank you," said Annabel Wallace. She talked!

"I have receipts for everything I spent on the trip. Much

of it I put on my American Express card. The only big unexpected expenses were renting a station wagon and paying a funeral director. If you do not wish to pay those, and I would certainly understand if you don't, I am sure I can get C. and the Oklahoma Bureau of Investigation to reimburse me."

I meant it as a half-joke. Or something like that.

She picked up a pen and opened a checkbook that she had brought to the room with her. They were lying on the glass coffee table between us.

"How much does it all come to, Mack?" she said, like she was paying Mack the Grocer.

"Sixteen hundred and thirty-seven dollars and eighty-two cents. That includes the car and the mortician, though. . . ."

"How much for you and your time?"

I have never been so insulted. Never. "Nothing for me. I am paid by the people of Oklahoma for what I do. Also, remember, Luther and I are friends."

She shrugged like you would at an upstart maid and began writing. There was a slight noise as she moved the felt-tip pen across the check, but there was no other sound. I had forgotten how long it takes to write out a check.

She tore it slowly out of the checkbook. *Pop-pop-pop* it went, like the sound of a toy cap gun. And she handed it to me.

"I hope you at least got a few good French meals out of it," she said.

"Yes, thank you."

She stood. C. and I stood. This thing was over. So much for Luther. Luther was over.

We followed her back through the long front hallways to the front door. I felt the need to say something else. So I said: "I know you are upset, Annabel. How could you be anything else? But that will pass. And some bright Oklahoma day, before you know it, you will look up and there will be Luther standing there. Whatever craziness he had will be out of his system and there he'll be, back to his old self, ready to resume his normal life as Luther. Don't give up hope. Whatever he's doing now, remember he is still Luther, the man you love, the man we all love and respect."

Annabel Wallace, her hand now on the front doorknob, turned to C.

"Mr. Hayes, if you ever hear that my husband has returned to this house, please be prepared to have a murder case on your hands. I will kill him. With my bare hands, probably."

"We're a death-penalty state, ma'am," C. said.

"Exactly," she said, and opened the door for us to pass through and out. Which we did.

11
. . .
PEARL
AND MARSHA

M Y EULOGY for Bobby Thornton is not worth repeating in detail. I just said a few things about his service in the U.S. Marines and his death in a foreign land named France during a heroic reenactment of the famous Okinawa march. I left unexplained why the first march was famous, why the reenactment was done in France instead of Okinawa and why grown-men adults like Bobby Thornton ran away to do it without a word to anyone. The funeral was at the Methodist church in Pawnee City. The sanctuary was full of people, which surprised me. I had developed the sure impression that Bobby Thornton was mostly an unloved and unhappy soul who probably had no friends. I felt guilty for thinking so when I looked out into the crowd of more than three hundred people of Pawnee City. As lieutenant governor, I attended and spoke at a lot of funerals for Oklahoma people I really did not know. This one was different. I had been there when this man died. Nobody else in that sanctuary had. It does make a difference. Sarah Thornton was right.

The most important thing about the funeral was Samuel Joseph Washington and what happened afterward.

Washington was the sole surviving Regular from the Red River bus. C. gave me his name and address in Sturant so I could go by there on the way back to Oklahoma City if I wanted to. I wanted to. I still very much ached to know why that bus had gone off that bridge. C. said the Texas and insurance people had pretty much closed the case as a Cause of Accident: Unknown.

Samuel Joseph Washington was an outside painter in Sturant who often rode Buck Vermillion's bus over the line to Denison to paint Texas outsides. His trips were so frequent that the Sturant bus depot people had put him on the Regulars list they'd given to the OBI. He was the one who had had the flu the day the bus went off the bridge. The OBI had found him but hadn't talked to him because, as C. reminded me, they couldn't think of anything to talk to him about. He doubted if I could, either.

I found Washington on a ladder. He was painting the outside of a new Circle of Love Doughnuts franchise store. It was a small drive-up place made mostly of wood on the outside, plastic on the inside. There were thousands of them, all identical, all over our part of the country. The company emblem was a huge chocolate-covered cake doughnut with a red heart in the center of the hole.

Washington was a black man in his thirties who clearly did not like talking to people like me, people who were white and who were in positions of authority. He would not come down from the ladder. He said his pay would be docked.

"When are you due for a break?" I asked.

"In a while," he replied. He kept his paintbrush moving. It was full of the distinctive quail-egg-blue paint the Circle of Love Doughnuts people used on all of their outsides.

Each of us was almost yelling in order to be heard by the other. It was a lot like some of the telephone conversations I had had with C. from France.

"I would like to know what it was like riding that eleven-ten bus to Denison," I said.

"It was late a lot, because it was a through bus from Chicago to Laredo," he said. "I never came across anyone on it who was going to Laredo, but that's what the sign in front always said on it."

"Were there a lot of people on there who rode it a lot like you?"

"They're all dead."

"I know. Yes, sir. Any of them seem to be special friends of the driver?"

There was a barely noticeable breath of a pause before he said, "Buck was friendly to all of us. Even us blacks. Good man, that Buck. I never heard him raise his voice to anybody. Even to drunks or old ladies who forgot where they were or where they were going or who they were. Buck insisted I call him Buck. Some of those white drivers would rather put a rope around my neck than hear me call them by their first names. Even in this day and time. Why don't you lieutenant governor–type people get together and stop that kind of attitude toward us instead of asking a lot of questions about good men like Buck? Do you let black people call you by your first name, Mr. Lieutenant Governor? I never met a lieutenant governor before. Do you like being it?"

Samuel Joseph Washington had not missed a stroke of his brush. Nor had he more than just barely glanced down at me since we started our high-volume conversation.

"Everybody, black and white, red and yellow, rich and poor, from Tulsa and the Panhandle, calls me Mack. Look at me. I'm a minority myself. Only have one eye."

He did not look at me. But he said, "One-eyed white people got one helluva bigger basket full of everything going for them than two-eyed black people."

"Okay, whatever. Tell me about the other regulars."

"Why, Mr. Lieutenant Governor?"

"Because I am trying to figure out why that bus went off that bridge, Mr. Washington, and I think it's possible that information about the Regulars might help. I don't know how or why, but who knows?" I unfolded the list of Regulars the depot had given the OBI.

"Anything special about Randolph Scott Power?"

"Nothing except he rode in from Utoka a couple of days a week to deposit money in Buck's wife's bank and then went on to Denison to see a sister."

194

"They've got banks in Utoka, why did he come to Sturant?"

"He said he didn't want anybody there, even at the bank, to know how much money he had."

"Did you believe him?"

That brought an interested glance down at me. "Yes, sir. I barely knew the man and he had no reason to lie and I had no reason to think he did."

"Louise Alma Richardson?"

"Never heard the name. Must be the little old white lady who never spoke to anybody except Buck. She was new and barely alive. She went to a doctor down in Sherman. Probably a bladder doctor. Nine-tenths of what ails old people has to do with their bladder. Did you know that?"

"No, sir. Jean Lou Stephenson."

He started to say something. Then stopped. And finally said, "Nice young woman. I never heard her last name."

"What else about her?"

"Nothing else about her."

I called out the names of two more men on the list. He offered little information about them. One had been a carpenter, who, like him, went to Denison for work; the other had worked in the Katy Railroad freight office in Denison. He lived in Sturant because his wife had a good job as a nurse at the Sturant Community Hospital.

I came back to Jean Lou Stephenson.

"You said she was nice. Nice in what way?"

"In every way."

"How friendly was she with Buck?"

There was a slight beat of hesitation. "No more, no less, than the rest of us. Except for Peggy. She's on there, too, isn't she?"

"Right. I was getting to her. What about her?"

"We all liked her. Too bad about her dying, so young and all. Pretty as a button."

"What else is there about her? Why did she ride the bus regularly? Where did she work?"

"You don't know?"

"No."

Another few beats of silence. "She worked at the bus depot. Selling tickets, you know, things like that."

"I guess you all knew her full name?"

"You bet. Peggy Ann Mosher. Everybody called her Peggy Ann."

I thanked him and left him to his painting the Circle of Love Doughnuts shop.

I had some work to do. There was no Peggy Ann Mosher on the Regulars list, and I had to find out why.

• • •

There are few things with a worse public image than a bus depot's. Just saying the words "bus depot" can cause people to shiver in fear of imagined drunks and panhandlers, sniff in disgust at imagined smells of puke and dirty urinals. Not for me. I happen to like those old depots, the older and grimier and stinkier the better, in fact. I joked with Fred Rayburn that maybe we should import some old urinal smells for his museum. But seriously. For me these depots were history, places where real people began and ended their very dramatic business of going from place to place, or as Continental Trailways said in its advertisements, "to the next town or across America." Although it was considered a good thing by most everyone else, I hated the fact that many of the old depots had been either remodeled spick-and-span or replaced altogether. Sturant's, unfortunately, was one of those. A really super rundown old one had been replaced by a tiny shiny new one right on the corner of Fifth and Sycamore, where U.S. 69-75 Business turned north out of town.

I made one stop before I got there, at a pay phone at a Conoco station. I called C. in Oklahoma City. It was a good Oklahoma connection, so both of us could talk in a normal conversational way.

"Did you say autopsies were performed on all twenty-four of the dead people on the bus or just on Buck Vermillion?" I asked.

"I don't think I said, because I don't think I know. What's up?"

"Can you find out if one was done on a passenger named Peggy Ann Mosher, who worked at the Sturant bus depot?"

"Why, Mack? What do you want to know about her? All of those people died of concussion things or by drowning or both."

"I still don't know *why* about any of this, C." Which

197

was true. I had no idea what I was aiming for—or at.

"Okay," he said, and I went on to the bus station.

. . .

There was still a black wreath hanging on the front door of the bus depot, which had been a Texaco station at one time. Now the small office had been fixed up with a tiny ticket counter and four black vinyl-and-chrome chairs for waiting passengers. A clock over the counter had neon around it that said: "To the Next Town or Across America." There was also a calendar that featured brown-and-white photos of buses through history. I had one like it in my office at the capitol. Hugh Glisan at the Oklahoma City depot had sent it to me.

One of the four chairs was occupied by a middle-aged man in work clothes reading a paperback book. A gray-haired woman in rimless glasses was behind the counter. I identified myself to her as the lieutenant governor of Oklahoma, as someone who happened to be around the day of the tragic Red River accident and as someone who along with Texas and other Oklahoma officials was still very interested in determining why that bus had gone off the bridge.

"Buck was drugged or shot, if you ask me, and I don't know why it's taking everybody so long to figure it out," she said. "All you have to do is watch the TV. I just never thought it would come to this part of Oklahoma. They're doing it every day everywhere in Oklahoma City and Tulsa. It's about time you and the others in charge do something about it. They wanted Buck's cash-fare money, I'll bet."

I decided there was no point in going through the autopsy report on Buck Vermillion. Or the lack of any other evidence that anybody had drugged or shot him.

"The loss of your ticket agent made it all the worse for you, I'm sure," I said, moving on to why I was there.

She reached for a handkerchief on the counter and said, "I loved that girl. Everybody who came in here loved Peggy Ann. I'll bet there were people who rode the bus just because they liked coming in here to buy tickets from her."

"I guess she was a local girl?"

"Grew up not six blocks from here, up by the college. Her momma, Pearl, was the best seamstress in town. Still is. She dressed up Peggy like she was from Tulsa, every day of the year."

"I noticed she was not on the Regulars list you gave the OBI."

The woman shook her head, wiped away a tear. "She wasn't a Regular. She never went anywhere on the bus. I was surprised to find out she was on that bus that morning. I saw her leave here in her car before the bus did, like she did every morning when her shift was over. Now that is a mystery how she got on that bus, to tell the truth."

I had no more questions for her. All of them now were for others. Including one more for Samuel Joseph Washington.

. . .

It was lunchtime. He was down off the ladder, sitting on the curb in front of the Circle of Love Doughnuts shop-to-be. He was eating what looked like a tunafish-salad sandwich on white bread. I loved tunafish sandwiches, but on wheat bread. In the old days my idea of heaven was one of those with a bag of narrow Fritos and a Grapette.

"Where did Peggy Ann get on the bus?" I asked.

"At the depot, like everybody else," he said, his eyes still on his sandwich.

"Again. Where did Peggy Ann get on the bus?"

"Why don't you leave it all alone?" he said. His tone was quiet and almost friendly, for a change. But very sad. "I wish I had never talked to you in the first place. I'm not saying any more."

"You want me to get a deputy sheriff to take you to the courthouse for a chat?"

He shook his head. "I'll bet you wouldn't treat a white like this."

"Yes, I would."

"She got on at the light at Seventh and Pine. On the way out of town. Buck stopped and opened the door and she hopped on."

"How often did it happen?"

He looked up at me now. "Please, no more. They were both good people to me."

I decided not to push it. Not with him.

·   ·   ·

I knew enough about bus companies and the way they operated to know that employees like Peggy Ann Mosher would have had an annual pass. She could ride a Continental Trailways bus free anytime she wanted to as long as there was an empty seat. But there had to be a pass slip filled out with her name and annual pass number that was put in the driver's trip report. Continental Trailways, like Greyhound and all the rest, occasionally put paid checkers incognito on their buses to make sure the actual head count of passengers jibed with the number of tickets, pass slips and cash fares the driver turned in at the end of his run. The main reason was to keep drivers from stealing cash fares paid by people without tickets who flagged buses along the highway. Buck Vermillion was without a doubt the kind of honest man who would take no chances. He would make sure there was a pass slip in his trip report for each and every time Peggy Ann Mosher rode his bus. No matter what else might have been going on.

The next morning, back in my office in Oklahoma City, I called Dean Brown, the tall vice-president for operations and safety for Continental Trailways in Dallas.

I asked him if he would mind pulling all of Buck Vermillion's trip reports for the last several weeks and months to see if there were a lot of pass slips for a Sturant ticket agent named Peggy Ann Mosher.

"She died in the crash, didn't she?" he said.

"Yes, sir."

"Some hanky-panky going on between them?"

"I don't know."

He was a bus man. He jumped to that conclusion because he knew as I did that bus drivers—some of them, at least—are in that great tradition of ship captains in the movies. To those guys, having girlfriends is as much a part of driving a bus as having a ticket punch on their right hip.

"Wouldn't solve the accident mystery even if there was, would it?" he said. "Never known layover sex yet to cause a man to lose control of a bus on a bridge."

"Good point . . ."

"Also, please remember we're talking about Buck Vermillion. The last man on earth who would play around. Hell, his wife's the president of the biggest bank in Sturant, for one thing. He's—was—as good as they come, for another. I'll check the trip reports and be back in touch."

I thanked him.

A short while later C. appeared at my office door. He had a manila file folder in his hand.

"They did autopsies on all of the dead," he said. "The Texas Department of Public Safety insisted. Wanted to rule out somebody being hopped-up crazy on drugs or something like that."

He walked over to my desk. "Do you want to read the report on Peggy Ann Mosher yourself, or do you want me to tell you?"

"Tell me."

"She was pregnant. Just a few weeks. It would have been a boy, according to the autopsy."

• • •

Dean Brown was back on the line from Dallas by the end of the afternoon.

"She went with him on that schedule once a week every

week beginning about six months ago," he said. "She went all of the way to Dallas and then she came back with him on his return schedule that afternoon."

"How long a layover in Dallas?" I asked, hoping that maybe Brown was the kind of man who could let 'layover' go by without some comment.

"Two and a half hours on the layover," he said. "Employees of Continental Trailways are permitted to lay over any way they wish, of course."

"Of course, Mr. Brown. Thank you."

"You think this adds up to something, don't you?"

"Yes, I do, frankly. I am still not sure what, but you would have to admit there could be a connection."

"Between her being pregnant and that Eagle going off the bridge? Forget it, Mr. Lieutenant Governor. Little women get pregnant every day from bus drivers. If that caused Continental Trailways buses full of people to sail off into the air, we'd have damn few buses still on the road."

He laughed. I didn't. "How did you know she was pregnant?" I asked.

"I have the same reports you do, sir. I have decided not to tell the world. What are your plans?"

"I don't know yet."

C. arranged for me to fly down to Sturant the next morning on the OBI Cessna.

· · ·

Pearl Mosher, Peggy Ann's mother, was in a wheelchair for reasons I did not know. It could have been something that happened just a few days before or back when she was born, for all I knew. She opened the door for me herself, though, and told me to follow her into her living room where we could talk. She had a gorgeous face. Big brown eyes, a small elegant nose, nice full lips, clear complexion. Her hair was dark gray. I guessed her age at about forty-five.

The room reminded me of my grandmother's living room in Coffeyville, Kansas. There were little white doily things on the arms of the chairs and couch, and photos of people in large wooden frames on the mantel over a fireplace with a small gas stove in it. One of the frames was draped with black ribbon. I went over and took a look. Peggy Ann Mosher was an exact replica of what her mother must have looked like when she was twenty or so years old.

It was terrible to think of her, pregnant, being thrown around to her death in that Continental Trailways Silver Eagle.

"Do you have any idea why that bus went off the Red River Bridge, Mrs. Mosher?" I said after some strained initial small talk.

She looked stunned by the question. Some color came to her face. "I am no expert on traffic accidents," she said. "Please, if you have come to ask me stupid questions like that I would just as soon you leave. I have much, much work to finish. . . ."

"Your daughter was single, wasn't she?" I asked.

"Yes."

"Did she have a regular boyfriend?"

"I do not have to talk to you about my daughter. She

is gone from me. Isn't that enough for me to deal with already? Go away, please."

"Certainly," I said, standing up. "I need to find Sycamore Street. Somebody said it was out north of the college football stadium. Is that right?"

"Yes," said Pearl Mosher, starting to roll out of the room. I casually moved to block her way.

"Where exactly," I said, "if you don't mind?"

"Go out the highway, turn left at Wilson . . ."

"Maybe you could draw me a rough map?"

I handed her a ballpoint pen and a spiral notebook turned to a blank page. Snorting with annoyance, she grabbed them and drew a few lines and wrote a few words like "Stadium," "Sycamore," "Wilson."

She handed the notebook back to me. I made a big thing of looking down at what she had drawn. Then I took an envelope out of my suitcoat pocket and, as she watched, unfolded the letter inside.

There was absolute silence for two or three very long seconds.

Then I said in my best lieutenant-governor-of-Oklahoma voice: "No question about it. The handwriting is identical."

I held the letter up to Mrs. Mosher's face so she could see it. But I really didn't have to. It was clear from the way she was staring that she knew what it was. And that she had been had. I had made the connection between her and the anonymous note C. had received about Buck's being a murderer.

"In what way did Buck Vermillion murder your daugh-

ter and those other people on that bus, Mrs. Mosher?" I
asked, changing my tone to that of an uncle.

Mrs. Mosher started crying. I offered her my handkerchief, which fortunately was still fresh and clean.

And after a while she told me the story she really
wanted to tell but on the other hand did not want to tell.
She said:

"He was thirty years older than she was. I went to high
school with Buck myself! He was married. His wife, who
I also went to school with, is president of a bank, and a
big shot in town. I do not know what got into Peggy Ann.
I do not understand it. But she fell for that old bus driver.
Sure, he was a handsome man back when he was young,
but not now. Not handsome enough for the likes of Peggy
Ann, at least. You saw her picture. Nobody prettier anywhere near here. When I was her age I couldn't have
imagined even looking at an old man like Buck. She never
did say it in so many words, but she started spending her
days off with him. I didn't know it for sure, but I really
did know it. She would go off with him on his bus to
Dallas and spend the day. I knew something like that was
happening. A few days before the accident, I finally said
something to her. I said, 'Honey, Buck Vermillion is not
right for you. He is wrong, oh, so wrong.' Well, she fought
me about it and said I was the one who was wrong and,
besides, he was going to marry her. I said Buck would
never leave Marsha at the bank. He was too upright for
that kind of thing. Oh, yes he would, she said. Just wait
and see. There was something nervous and funny about

her for a couple of days before the accident. I don't know, but I really do know that my baby finally pressed Buck to do something, so he killed her."

"Do you have any evidence of that at all?" I asked.

"Doesn't it add up that way to *you*? Isn't that why you're here?"

"Well, it's certainly a possibility. It's still hard to understand why a man would take his own life and that of so many others in the process."

"You don't know Buck Vermillion. It's the upright good people who do the crazy things like this. They'd rather kill a dozen and be dead themselves than have people know they're just as rotten and bad as the rest of us."

I thought of Luther and the boys in France. And Bobby Thornton in the ground over at Pawnee City.

The OBI agent from the Sturant office who was driving me around had a message for me when I got back to the car. Mrs. Vermillion at the bank would love for me to come by while I was in town. If it was convenient.

. . .

Going from Pearl Mosher in her wheelchair to Marsha Vermillion behind her desk at the bank was like going over the state line from Texarkana, Texas, to Texarkana, Arkansas. Or vice versa. Those two women lived in the same town but in very different worlds.

Marsha Vermillion's bank president's office was just like every other bank president's office I had ever been in. Heavy dark wood furniture and bookcases. Giant glass ashtrays, framed certificates and diplomas, silver gavels and autographed pictures of important Oklahoma people. I don't know what I had expected, but I hadn't expected it to be like all the others. Jackie's office, for instance, is certainly not like any male company president's. It is full of modern furniture and cleanliness and pastels and chrome.

Marsha Vermillion shook my right hand, looked into my one good eye and guided me toward a chair in front of her desk. I watched her carefully as she walked around her huge desk and sat down. This was one very big, tough woman. I am ashamed to confess that is was not hard at all for me to understand why Buck Vermillion, whom I had never met, took up with a pretty little thing like Peggy Ann Mosher. I could not defend it but I could understand it. Marsha Vermillion clearly was not a pretty little thing and never had been.

As we made small talk I was overcome with confusion and uncertainty about what I should and would say to this woman. I wished I had insisted C. come with me. Or waited until he could and would. Or called him after I left Pearl Mosher's. Or not come at all.

"I wonder if you would send me a photograph for my collection?" she said. "Autographed, of course. It would be an honor to have the lieutenant governor represented over there."

She looked off to her left at a wall of autographed black-and-white eight-by-ten photos, about thirty-five or forty in all. I recognized several sheriffs and OU football players and a couple of state senators, including Hank Lauter, the pusher of the Adabel–Sturant turnpike. There were also at least two country singers, one of them being Nita Pickens of Perkins Corner.

"Nita Pickens and I appeared together at an Oklahoma Southeastern commencement a few years back," I said.

"Which one of you sang?" She laughed. And I laughed. Very funny, Mrs. Vermillion.

"Well, tell me if you can, is there anything new about the accident?" she said quickly, before I could say anything else mundane. I was an important person, all right, but she was busy and there were obviously other things on her bank president's schedule for the day. Can't waste the day away talking to the lieutenant governor of Oklahoma. No sirree!

"Not really, ma'am. The major investigation is being conducted by Texas."

"I understand you paid a visit to the mother of one of the victims. Little Peggy Ann Mosher's mother. Buck and I went to school with Pearl. She was quite a beauty before her accident. She broke her back in the fire, as you probably know."

I gave her a dumb look, signaling the fact that I did not know. And she went on.

"She and Tommy Mosher, Peggy Ann's father, lived in a big two-story house out north of town. There was a fire. She was up there on the second floor and she jumped.

Landed the wrong way. It was a terrible thing. Tommy burned up because he wouldn't jump until she did, and by the time she did it was too late for him. Buck and I always liked him. His middle name was Templeton. Tommy Templeton Mosher. The Templetons were from Colbert. There's still some there. We've loaned them money for cars and farms. No Moshers left, though. Except Pearl. Wonder where Peggy Ann was headed on that bus that morning? Buck told me she had gone to work at the bus station."

I had nothing to say. She went on.

"I wish you could have known Buck, Mr. Lieutenant Governor. He was a fine man with a fine reputation. I am sure nothing will come out of this accident to change that. Would you like a cup of coffee? I am so sorry I did not offer you one when you came in," She was standing now.

I stood and said, "No, thank you. I have to get back to Oklahoma City."

"What brought you here today?"

"Oh, nothing special."

"Certainly not just to see Pearl Mosher."

"Certainly not," I said, thinking on my feet. For a change. "There's more on that turnpike business to look into."

"That may be the most ridiculous idea in the history of Oklahoma government," she said. "It is an insult to suggest we have a two-lane turnpike. I have never heard of such a thing. You go back and tell that crazy governor we either should have a real one with four lanes or none at all. Don't you agree?"

"Well, these things have a way of sorting themselves out, here in our democratic form of Sooner government, Mrs. Vermillion."

And we said our good-byes.

12
· · ·

OKLAHOMA TACO EXPRESS

WHILE I was away in France, C. had grown tired of pizza and had turned to fast-food tacos. Tacos with chicken and guacamole. Tacos with ground meat, cheese, lettuce and tomatoes. Tacos with shrimp and mushrooms. Tacos with everything imaginable. He said with enthusiasm that Oklahoma City now had drive-thru restaurants from which it was possible to get 123 different kinds and combinations of tacos.

"I don't like tacos that much, C.," I said.

"Neither did I when I started," he replied. "But I do now."

It was the next day and we were in the backseat of his car on the way to Oklahoma Taco Express #5–Northside for lunch so I could brief him on what I had found out in Sturant. We also had not had that much time to talk about France and Luther and other things.

"She didn't say anything about her being pregnant," he said of Buck's wife. "Why didn't you?"

"I think she already guessed, but if she didn't I got to wondering why she needed to ever know, and decided if that time should come we could tell her then."

C. shrugged as if to say, Maybe you did the right thing, maybe you didn't, who knows? He said: "What do you think happened to that bus, Mack?"

"I think he intentionally drove it off the bridge to keep Peggy Ann quiet about the two of them and about her being pregnant."

"She must have been really putting it on him to marry her or do something."

"He did something, all right."

"Makes Luther's running away sound like a more reasonable way of solving things, doesn't it?" I said.

I had an urge to say Buck and Luther were alike in some way, that what they felt and did connected in some way. I did not say it, because I was not sure I could explain what I felt or meant to C. or to anyone else.

We kept talking and eventually got around to it, anyway.

C. said: "What do we do with what we think happened with the bus?"

"What is there to do?"

"Probably nothing," he said. "It's all theory, and at this point who needs to know besides the two of us. You agree?"

"Agreed."

I had what the drive-thru menu called a Tuscany Italian Taco Treat. A silly name for a silly something to eat. All it was was a taco stuffed with ground meat and spaghetti sauce and melted provolone cheese. It was truly awful.

"Do you believe Luther's need-to-be-crazy-and-irresponsible story?" I said as we ate and cruised the streets of Oklahoma City. C. had gotten the Taco Skyscraper, which was a taco twice the normal size stuffed with about fifteen different ingredients—from dill pickles and turkey to mayonnaise and chili. It made me almost sick just watching him eat the thing.

"I believe it," C. said, "because there's nothing else to believe, because nothing else makes even as much sense as that."

He asked me about the Methodist nympho business. I told him about Moe Hancock.

"Well, they're still looking for him," he said. "The latest MP bulletin has a full profile, and it gives one of his characteristics as just what you found out. It said he was known for his great storytelling."

I had the sudden wonder. Was that whole terrible story about little Moe Two another of Hancock's great stories? No! Nobody would do that. Particularly the Methodist bishop of North Carolina. But on the other hand, I wanted it to be a lie.

C. said: "I guess there's no responsible middle-aged man I know who doesn't occasionally want to throw it all over, Mack. To just up and turn the other way when he gets to his street, and keep going. To be crazy and

irresponsible for a change. It's human nature and it's normal. Luther just acted on it, which is not normal."

"I know, I know. The cop out in Kansas City told me
the same thing. He said everybody wants to just keep
driving. Everybody but me. So far at least," I said. And
it was true.

"Just think what it would be like if all of the responsible
middle-aged men of Oklahoma and America started running away like Luther and Buck."

"I'm going to do it myself if I ever have to eat another
Tuscany Italian Taco Treat."

"It'll grow on you. I promise. Before long you'll be
having a Skyscraper with me, just like it's routine."

He opened his mouth wide and took a huge, noisy bite
of his huge, crunchy taco. Tiny bits of shredded cheddar
cheese and fried onion and diced tomato fell into the
Oklahoma Taco Express paper plate on his lap. Small
drools of chili juice and mayonnaise appeared on his chin.

I gagged and looked away and down at my watch. It
was 11:45 in the morning, Oklahoma time, which meant
it was 6:45 in the evening, France time.

I tried to imagine what the crazy people were doing
in La Napoule.

I told C. in detail about the march and Luther and his
friends and the death of Bobby Thornton. We agreed that
maybe we should no longer regret so much that our de-
formities had kept us out of the armed forces.

And finally, as we got back to the capitol parking lot,
we got around to the turnpikes and Joe's idiotic plan to

build two two-lane ones. C. said it was without a doubt
the dumbest thing The Chip had ever done and that, he
said, was like talking about which was wetter—oceans or
lakes.

I said to C.: "Well, you can relax. I have an appointment
with Joe for two o'clock this afternoon. I'm going to kill
those turnpikes once and for all, for the good of this state
and its people."

"How in God's name are you going to do that?"

"If I told you that, you would know all of my secrets."

. . .

I never crossed Joe. Not to his face, at least. I had
sometimes worked around his edges to counter some
things I did not think were in the interests of Oklahoma,
but I had never taken him on directly. He was the governor, I was the lieutenant governor. We were elected as
a team and we served as a team. Always. No matter what.

So it was as a member of the team that I spoke the
words that brought death to those two turnpikes. Both of
them. The killer words I spoke in his office a few minutes
after two o'clock that afternoon were:

"I just talked to Luther. He's thinking about coming
home. Maybe tomorrow."

Joe was on his feet. His face was red. "Why, why? No!
You told me I could bank on it. Bank on it, you said.
What happened? What happened?"

"It's the turnpikes, Joe. Somebody, probably some
trouble-making Republican on the Senate side, called him
in France and told him about your two-lane idea. Luther

said there should be no new turnpikes of any number of lanes, but two lanes is simply outrageous. He said it is the only thing that could make him come home to fight you. He said never in his years in state government had he heard of anything so wrongheaded and stupid, so idiotic and ill conceived, so worth summoning all of the resources at his disposal to kill. . . ."

Halfway through all this, Joe slumped down in his chair. Now he sat silent for a count of three.

Then he said, "You know I can't do it with Luther back, don't you, Mack?"

"I know, Joe," I said.

Joe sat some more, and then he sighed. "You know who else I heard from today? Marsha Vermillion. Runs a bank down in Sturant? Always raises money for the Party? She called and said that if we made the turnpike a two-lane, she'd personally guarantee the Democratic Party of Oklahoma never saw another dime from Sturant again. Said it was better to forget the whole thing. I can't understand it, Mack. These people just have no vision."

He sat straight up. He had made a decision.

So long, turnpikes.

"You say they have telephones where Luther is?" Joe asked.

"Sure," I replied. "I used them myself."

"And you can get through from here to there in our kind of English?"

"Sure."

Joe nodded. "Then call Luther and tell him to stay put.

Tell him it's over. No new turnpikes, two-lane or any other kind of lane. Tell him it's over. He can stay right where he is."

"Are you sure, Joe?"

"I was sick of fighting about turnpikes, anyhow."

Right. And I had counted on his short attention span. And on his preferring that Luther never came back to Oklahoma for any reason whatsoever. But that little call from Marsha Vermillion was an unplanned, unexpected piece of giant luck.

But maybe football coaches are right when they say the good ones make their own luck.

· · ·

I left Joe's office feeling funny, though. Something was wrong. First I thought it was what I had just done to Joe. I had lied to him about Luther's coming back. I hated to lie, but sometimes it was necessary. I had sworn to uphold the Constitution and laws of Oklahoma and to do what I believed was right. So how could I do anything but step in and stop that crazy turnpike idea?

No, it was not Joe and turnpikes. It was Buck and Luther. There was something about my adventures with the two of them and all their various friends and relatives that was caught somewhere in me. In my throat, in my soul, in my something.

So I went to the National Motor Coach Museum to think about it. To be alone.

Fred Rayburn had used some money inherited from a rich lady passenger to found the museum. But nobody came and it did not prosper, even after he dropped the thirty-five-cent admission charge and made it free. Now he opened it a few Saturday mornings in the summer and fall and otherwise only by appointment, which was rare. But with my key, I could go anytime I wished.

I went right to the mock-up of the driver's compartment from a 1944 Aerocoach, the latest addition to the museum. That was the great thing about Fred. He did not let the fact that nobody came to his museum stop him from acquiring new things. The Aerocoach was a bus made mostly just before, during and after World War II. It had a flat front end, thirty-seven seats and a most unusual gearshift lever on the floor by the driver's seat. The knob was silver, perfectly round and the size of a baseball. There was a little button set in the top that had to be pushed before shifting straight back to reverse.

Fred had found an Aerocoach in a junkyard somewhere up in Iowa. He had the driver's seat, the steering wheel and column, the dashboard and some of the other basics dismantled and brought to Oklahoma City for realistic reassembly. He planned for this and three other driver's compartments from other buses to provide a way for kids to sit behind the steering wheel of a bus and, he hoped, get turned on to being bus drivers. Unfortunately, not many little boys were interested in becoming bus drivers anymore. As I said, there were few people of any age, aside from professional bus people, who were interested in any of Fred's vast collection of old depot signs, driver's cap badges, model buses, coin changers, ticket punches, ticket validators, bus café china and silverware, and all the rest.

I slipped into the Aerocoach's driver's seat. The steering wheel was mounted on a column that came up from a solid block of wood on the floor. The wheel was a beautiful ivory color. It had the look and touch of porcelain. I put both hands on it and turned it to the right and then to the left.

How could Buck have given the wheel a hard pull to the right and sent that Trailways Silver Eagle through that guardrail? And sent that girl from the bus station and all of the others to their deaths? What about the girl? Didn't he love her at all? She was pregnant. How could Buck not have given at least a split second's thought to whether that baby was going to be a boy or a girl?

Not to mention himself. He also killed himself, for God's sake. I tried to understand how he could have done it. I just couldn't.

I grabbed the silver-knobbed gearshift lever and moved it into first gear. Like I was about to drive that Aerocoach out and away to somewhere. To somewhere way, way far away from Oklahoma?

Hey, how much fun it would be to drive this thing right down the main street of La Napoule. I could find those crazies and say, Okay, Luther, Preacher and you other guys. Here I am. Here I am! Get aboard and let's go somewhere. I'm back just for a while. I'll go home again someday. Maybe tomorrow even. But just for a while let's go for a bus ride.

All aboard!

My hands started shaking there on that porcelain steering wheel.

I sat there for more than a half-hour like a crazy man, driving that bus around France and places, moving the wheel around to the right and then to the left, occasionally shifting the gears from first, to second, third and fourth. And into reverse.

Finally, whatever it was that had come over me passed, and I went back to the capitol, back to being who I was.

I thought it was too bad Luther wasn't there. I would have told him that someday all of us one-eyed lieutenant governors in the world might get together and run away to some place far away, like he and his buddies had done.

Only without that crazy hiking. *We* would ride an old Aerocoach everywhere we went.